MOURNING Heaven

AMY LANE

Dreamspinner Press

Published by
Dreamspinner Press
5032 Capital Circle SW
Ste 2, PMB# 279
Tallahassee, FL 32305-7886
USA
http://www.dreamspinnerpress.com/

Mourning Heaven
Copyright © 2012 by Amy Lane

Cover Art by Paul Richmond
http://www.paulrichmondstudio.com

ISBN: 978-1-61372-745-4

Printed in the United States of America
First Edition
September 2012

eBook edition available
eBook ISBN: 978-1-61372-746-1

For Mate, who has yet to fall down on the job.

AUTHOR'S NOTE ON THE BOSS

WHEN I was in sixth grade, my best friend, Stacy Muir, played "Thunder Road" for me from a bootlegged tape her brother had made at a concert.

It was one of the most beautiful songs I'd ever heard.

Bruce Springsteen has been one of my biggest inspirations as a writer. He writes about little people with little stories, and for a brief span of music and lyrics, he makes those little people my entire world. He has turned his band into his family, and every one of them has a voice. His songs are about dreams and loyalty and kindness and cruelty and about how sometimes, when people are broken, they just can't be fixed.

When I grow up, I want to be just like him.

This novel started when I was listening to Bruce Springsteen songs, in particular "Gypsy Biker," "Devil's Arcade," "Magic," "Last to Die," and "I'll Work For Your Love," which are all on the *Magic* CD. I wanted to write a book that made me feel like those songs for the *entire* length of the book. Of course, after writing *Mourning Heaven*, I now know why Bruce writes about his people in two- to three-minute songs, because that much pain might just kill you dead if you live it for too long, but mostly, I hope I succeeded in capturing for you what he has given to me.

Thank you, Bruce. You may never ever read this or even know there's a writer like me out there, living your art in her very soul, but I owe you an awful goddamned lot. Maybe even enough to forgive you for not seeing me during the *Born in the USA* tour when I was eighteen and absolutely positive that you'd see me in the nosebleed seats with the thirty thousand other people in the Oakland Coliseum and know that we were destined to be together forever. It's okay, buddy. You picked a redhead in the end—you must have felt me out there somehow.

—Amy

TELEGRAM

Daisy, California. Population 2,726.

WHEN Peter Armbruster moved there when he was ten, it became 2,727. Children were born, old folks died, a few folks moved in. When Peter's cousin, Michael, died in Afghanistan twelve years later, it was 2,813. Wait, no—2,812.

Because you had to count Bodi.

A month before he'd shipped out, Michael snuck his mom's car out of the garage to help Bodi move all of his stuff from the bedroom of his old house to nobody-knew-where-at-the-time. As far as Peter knew, they went out the bedroom window, because Bodi's mother wouldn't have let Michael in her house right then, and Bodi himself was lucky all his shit didn't end up on her lawn. The roar of Bodi's Harley Davidson at two in the morning was pretty much the last anyone in Daisy knew for sure about where Bodi had gone—anyone except Peter. Peter had kept track. Bodi showed up in Arcata not much later, where he had opened a machine shop and was living in a flat above it, according to rumors. Although Peter was never sure of the identity of the occasional Daisy resident who had seen him, Peter knew that's where he'd gone. Peter had checked those rumors out himself. He dreamed about Bodi in those six years, and always, always, he was somewhere other than Daisy, and he was happy.

The day Peter's aunt Aileen got the news about Michael, she sat down abruptly on her front porch—not on the swinging seat behind her but on the boards. It wasn't a collapse, per se, just a simple statement that she would take this news on her own terms,

1

and Peter tried hard not to think bitter things such as that was how she expected the rest of the world had to live its life too: on her terms.

Peter helped her up and took the telegram from her nerveless fingers and then walked her into the house. Later, he'd start the neighborhood phone tree, wherein he'd call her best friend, who lived a mile away, and her parents—his grandparents—who lived down in Sacramento, and they would spread the word. Eventually, even Michael's father, who lived up in Crescent City, would hear, although he didn't bother to show up at the funeral.

But in the meantime, it was only Peter James Armbruster and Aileen Catherine Armbruster in the silence of the house they'd shared for over eleven years. It had been that long since Peter's mother had brought him to Daisy. He'd been ten, and his mother had been exhausted and grieving. Even if she didn't have the means to raise him, she did have the love.

They'd heard from Ginnifer since then: she often showed up on Peter's birthday, bearing cards and stories, and Peter had learned to love those visits—but also not to expect them. The last time she'd been there, she'd managed to hold on to a job and a boyfriend for a couple of months, and Peter could sense the relief in her, because the gypsy life she'd led hadn't been of her choosing but more thrust upon her. Peter actually had more of a life in Daisy by then, and he hadn't begged to go with her. He'd spent his first two years as a child pleading to leave with her. After Bodi arrived, he'd stopped begging, but just because he felt like he had chains that bound him to the wormshit of a mountain town didn't mean that his mother's absence hadn't hurt.

And those chains that bound him hadn't offered much comfort, either. After Michael had shipped out, it had mostly been just Peter and Aileen, echoing around in the big yellow two-story house that sat a block back from Zinnia Street, the main drag through Daisy.

Although it was maybe seventy-five miles from the ocean, Daisy was close enough to the foothills of Highway 120 to sit in the red dirt of the mountains. The dusty ochre-colored sunshine filtering through the blinds in the west-facing window tinted all of Peter's thoughts and memories. That sanguine shade of light was omnipresent. It shined on the day his mother left him in Daisy, it shined on the day Bodi had left, and that light would forever bleed on the day when they found out Michael's life had ended.

"Say it!" Aileen snapped as Peter put the kettle on the stove and, conversely, set about getting some ice in a glass. Ice water first, tea second. He had no idea why that made sense.

"Say what," he muttered tonelessly. He knew what she was talking about, but he didn't want to talk about it. His own mind was running a nonstop film loop of Michael, as Peter had known him. Michael had been four years older than Peter. When Peter had arrived in Daisy, Michael had been every bit as lonely living in that house as Peter had been in the six years since Michael had left. Peter had been an instant little brother for Michael. And Michael?

Michael had set Peter's sun and his moon and his stars. He'd painted the sky black for the deep summer nights and initiated the breeze that breathed through Peter's window into his sweltering attic room. Michael, with his dark, curly hair and his deep brown/green eyes (his father's eyes—Aileen never let him forget it), had been everything Peter wanted to be. For Peter's first two years in Aileen's house, Michael had been Peter's everything, and for the next four years, he'd been the other half of Peter's everything.

And then he'd been gone.

"Say that I killed him," Aileen spat now, wringing her thin, dry hands. She'd been pretty once. She had. She'd had blonde hair and a lively face, a wide smiling mouth, and sparkling blue eyes. By the time Peter had gotten there, she'd been middle-aged at thirty-four. Now she was ancient in her forties.

"A land mine killed him," Peter said without emotion. "Just ask the DOD."

"That's not what you're thinking," Aileen snapped. She was crying. Her voice wasn't breaking, and she wasn't sobbing, but her eyes were red and her nose was swollen and there were tracks down the faint sheen of dust on her lean face.

"If I knew what I was thinking, Aunt Aileen, I'd tell you," Peter said with resignation. For a moment, he watched his fingers pick at the cheap laminate on the wooden counter. He closed his eyes tight and saw Michael as he had been the morning before their entire world had fallen apart. He'd been happy that day: his face had been flushed and his hair had been tousled. Peter had been the only one to know why, but his smile—white teeth in a tanned face and green/brown eyes that crinkled in the corners, inviting people in—had been transcendent. Michael Hickham (unlike his mother, he'd kept his father's name) had wanted the entire world to be as happy as he was. Peter had managed, too, at great personal cost to himself, to be as happy as Michael that day. He'd worshipped his cousin. He wouldn't have deprived him of a thing in the world.

"You're thinking I killed him," Aileen said again, and she wiped her cheek with the back of her hand. "You'd be right," she whispered. "You'd be right. But I didn't make him go on that second tour. I didn't make him go enlist."

Peter swallowed. "You didn't tell him it was all right, either."

He walked out of the kitchen then and called her best friend, proud of the way his voice was steady and he kept the tears out. Joelle was over in less than five minutes, still wearing an apron and dragging her seven-year-old by the arm. Aileen fell into her friend—who was one of those lively, bosomy women who made *everybody* feel at home—and sobbed on her shoulder while Lucy sat, bewildered, on Aileen's green flowered couch.

Peter went in to check on the little girl, turned on the television, and found a cable station with kids' shows on it.

"What happened?" Lucy asked, looking into the kitchen, where her mom was holding Peter's aunt Aileen like a little girl.

"My cousin died," Peter said.

"Aren't you sad?" the little girl asked. She had straight brown hair with a little pink bow in it on the side. She was wearing cut-off

4

shorts with sparkles in the pockets and a pink halter top, and had skinned knees. She was completely secure in the little world of Daisy, knew she could ask questions and be exactly who she was and the world would adore her. Peter wished to hell he had ever been that unselfconscious about anything in the world.

"Yeah," he said, not wanting to think about it.

"Then why aren't you crying?"

"'Cause I'm not ready yet," he said.

When Michael was sixteen and Peter was twelve, Michael took Peter into the garage to work on his motorcycle. They'd spent a lot of time in that garage in the two years since Peter had first arrived at Daisy, but Peter was going through a growth spurt and was, like a lot of kids that age, clumsy as hell. He tripped on the toolbox on the floor and sliced his left hand open on the uncovered circular saw that sat in the corner. Michael was appalled.

"Jesus fucking Christ, Peter James. What in the fuck were you trying to do?" Michael literally ripped the T-shirt off his own back and wrapped it around the cut, which was gaping widely in anticipation of blood.

"That's weird, Mikey," Peter said, looking detachedly as the blood began to seep through the T-shirt. "It doesn't even hurt at all."

"Yeah, give it a fucking minute," Michael half laughed. Later Peter would figure out that he was fighting hysteria, but then, the exasperation had been comforting. Peter would be okay if Michael could still laugh. "Here, you come sit in Mom's car, and I'll go get the keys and drive you to Crescent City, okay?"

Crescent City was forty miles away, but it had a small med clinic, and Peter could get stitches there.

"Will it hurt when we get there?" Peter asked, his voice faint and far away.

"Yeah, Petey—it'll hurt like a motherfucker. Don't worry. You're not gonna get away that easy."

Halfway to Crescent City, he'd been fighting tears. By the time they'd gotten there, he'd stopped fighting.

So now Peter sat on the couch and blindly watched SpongeBob SquarePants and wondered when the pain was going to start.

PEOPLE came and comforted Aileen. Half the town gathered in the front room and brought casseroles and cakes and cornbread, and Peter moved silently in and out, stacking dishes, cleaning up, wrapping food, making note of whom to write a thank-you note to and who got the casserole dish when they were done.

By eight o'clock someone had given Aileen a Xanax and put her to bed, and Peter grabbed his denim jacket (because it was early spring and there was a chill in the air yet) and the keys to his little ages-old Toyota Corolla and slid out the side door from the kitchen.

"Where you going?" Joelle asked, and she was tired, too, and her voice was short. "Your auntie needs you!"

"I'll be back before she wakes up," he said, although Arcata was nearly a hundred miles away.

"So your cousin's dead and you're just going to take off all night? That woman *raised* you!" Joelle snapped.

Peter looked at her, wondering where all of that warmth that he'd seen at the kitchen table had gone. He needed it now, oh God, yes he did, but he knew better than to expect anything from this town when he needed it. He'd had a roof over his head and food on his table, clothes on his back, and Michael, whom he'd loved. He'd had everything he'd needed, and the town wasn't going to give him one more thing.

"I'll be back before she wakes up," he repeated. "This won't take long."

"What's so damned important that you need to do it right goddamned now?" Joelle's eyes were unattractively small when she squinted them like that. She was much prettier when she was a big blowsy white woman, radiating sunshine and goodwill.

"Someone's got to tell Bodi," he said, his blood throbbing at him to get out that door. "It's only right."

"You think his mama hasn't already done that?" Joelle asked, and Peter shrugged.

"Not if she's anything like Aunt Aileen, she hasn't."

Joelle's attitude dropped from her like a comfortable coat, and what was left was bare and uneasy. "All right. I'll stay here 'til you get back."

"Thank you," he said, and he was gone, thinking that the truth was, he couldn't have stayed in that house one more goddamned minute and kept dragging one breath in after another. If Joelle hadn't been there, he would have left his aunt alone to whatever solace she could find in a bottle of pills.

THERE was probably a specific geographic line for when the thick redwoods and foliage of Klamath National Forest gave way to the rolling hills and soft greens by the ocean, but Peter had, for every day since he'd arrived on Aileen and Michael's doorstep, managed to be elsewhere in his head when he passed it. He just knew that the world got... better. One minute it seemed you couldn't roll down the window without choking on the closeness of the woods, and the next, you rolled down the window and wore the smell of yarrow and salt on your skin. The wind was constant, and it always came off the water, even if the water was five miles away, and it always smelled of... better. Better places, better things, better times.

And once Peter reached the twisting, cliff-twined, rock-fraught passage of Highway 1 and turned south, he was going toward Arcata—and even before Bodi had moved there, becoming Daisy legend, Arcata had held a special significance for Peter. Arcata had been Peter's Holy Grail. Arcata had housed that magical place called "school."

"MOM, why can't we?" It was the summer before Peter started high school, and Michael's voice echoed up the stairs straight to Peter's room. Until the day before Michael had enlisted, neither Michael nor Aileen had realized that a conversation in the kitchen carried all the way up the stairs, but for Peter, it was comforting. No matter what the adults around him were doing, he had a warning system in place. He heard Aileen talk about Ginnifer Armbruster's drug habit, lament that nobody knew who his father was, and complain bitterly about Michael's father and how the bastard could never do more than send the bare minimum child support.

"Why can't we what?" Aileen's voice was sharp. She was baking for church the next day. Peter had helped her, quietly, after he'd gotten home from the chess club meeting, but she still had a lot to do. He didn't know why she'd sent him to bed early—maybe he'd just gotten on her nerves.

"Why can't we send him to college?"

"That money in the bank's for *you*, Michael, not for *him*!"

"Yeah, but I'm not going to use it!" Michael said, and his voice was firm—firmer than Peter had ever heard it.

"What the hell do you think you're going to do besides go to college?" Her irritated question was accompanied by the dropping of a cookie tray on the table, and Peter longed desperately for a cookie. He'd asked for one, after he'd helped, and that's when she'd sent him to bed. He lay there, smelling the cookies, thinking resentfully that if she wanted him to listen to what she said all the damned time, maybe she'd better start giving him cookies.

"Bodi and I are going to start a machine shop," Michael said excitedly. "We're going to fix motorcycles and do custom work. Bodi's uncle already taught him all the basics, and he's been showing me—"

"Yeah, remember where that got us? Peter's hand all sliced up. Sixteen stitches, Michael—do you have any idea what that doctor bill was?"

"Yeah, Mom. You've told me enough times. I'm sorry, okay? It was an accident. I'm just saying that—"

"And I don't want you hanging out with that Kovacs kid. There's rumors about that boy—"

"What? That he takes care of his little sister?"

"His retarded little sister. How do you think she got that way?"

"Brain damage from an accident. And she's nice, Mom. Stop calling her retarded—it sounds mean."

"Yeah, whatever. That boy is funny. Everyone in town is saying so. Do you know what he checks out of the library?"

"Yeah, I do, but I'm his best friend. What business is it of yours?"

"Poetry. And not just any poetry—"

"Ovid's love poems." Michael's voice dropped, became a little dreamy. "They're beautiful, Mom. I want Petey to read them. He'd totally get them—"

"That kid has enough problems!" Aileen snapped. "Look at him—he's skinny, he's girl-pretty—people keep telling me he's a fag. He's going to get the shit kicked out of him in school!"

"No," Michael said grimly. "Not anymore."

Lying in bed, Peter had a sudden epiphany. Michael picked him up from school twice a week. Toward the middle of eighth grade, Michael had picked him up off the ground a couple of times after he'd gotten thrown in a trash can or been tripped in a mud puddle or had his lunch ground down his shirt. The second week this had happened, Bodi had been in the car and had helped Michael bandage Peter's knuckles, because Peter did put up a fight. There were just more of them, and they were bigger.

One day the week after that, all of those kids came to school with black eyes and fat lips, and the torture stopped. Peter had always suspected that it had been Michael, and now he knew—

"What do you mean? What did you do?"

"Not me. It was Bodi." Michael's voice held justifiable pride. "Bodi got pissed. He sees enough of that shit going on with his sister. He doesn't put up with it—not for her, and not for Petey. It's not a crime to be somebody this town has never seen before, Mom. And that's what I'm saying about Petey—"

"He can't have your college money, Michael. That's yours."

"I don't want it. Bodi already has start-up from a bank down in Eureka. He's already got a client base just working at the garage in town. I've been helping him for a year, we're going to—"

"You're going to stop hanging out with that kid!"

"I'm almost eighteen. You're going to stop telling me who my friends are."

Michael didn't get mad. Not really. His voice just assumed this almost unearthly calm, the sort of calm of a big bank of clouds about ready to unleash hell. Not even Aileen was immune when her son sounded like that, and her next words were almost placating.

"Just remember, Michael, people around here think a lot of you. You wouldn't want to ever let them down."

"I wish you'd worry less about the people around town and more about the people under your own roof. Peter is really fucking smart. He's smarter than the teachers—hell, I think he checks Mr. Szabo's math for him. And he's talented. Have you seen the models he's made of the solar system or—"

"None of that is going to get him a real job, Michael!"

"The hell it's not! Who do you think designs all that shit we have in the classroom or the library, Mom? Science sculpting is big work!"

"Well, it's nice to dream, but when he's a grown-up, he's going to want something to fall back on. Joelle's husband said he can wait tables when he's ready."

Michael's voice almost broke then. "Mom, if you're not going to do anything for him when he graduates, I will. He can come live with Bodi and I in Crescent City or Arcata. We'll be set by then. I don't want him to stay here if that's the only kind of life you want for him—"

"It's a fine kind of life," Aileen said, like she was talking to a bothersome child. Like she was talking to Peter.

"It's a life of giving up," Michael said. There was the sound of the kitchen screen door slamming and Aileen calling after him ineffectually.

"Michael! Michael, tomorrow's church! Don't go off with that boy when we've got church tomorrow! Michael!"

But no, Michael was not at church the next day. The Sunday afterward, Peter skipped out on church too, and followed him, and found out why.

DETRITUS OF LEAVE

PETER drove into Arcata about twice a month, ostensibly to stock up for his aunt at the larger supermarket, but that wasn't the real reason.

The real reason was to look at the college.

Humboldt State University was actually on the small side, but Peter didn't care. He'd gotten a free catalog every semester and circled the classes he was going to take and highlighted the routes he'd walk on the college campus. He'd get his savings account readouts and calculate: books, semester tuition, rent. Yes. He'd priced the local student housing too. He wasn't going to commute to school, no. He was going to move out with a year's worth of rent and three years' worth of tuition, and he was going to work his way through college—he had maybe six months to go. He was going to learn about the world, learn about the far side of the sea, get the holy fuck out of his suck-ass town.

The fact that he'd figured out where Bodi lived and worked was a plus to learning about Arcata—but it wasn't the only reason he'd memorized the town's layout by heart.

The machine shop was a little off the main drag, right next to a Big O Tires store and on the other side of a muffler shop. "Gypsy Biker" was the hand-painted sign above the shop, and it had been repainted recently. The entire storefront was tidy, and even the lot had been swept, which was more than Peter could say for the Big O and the muffler shop.

There was a set of stairs—and again, they looked new—that went up the back to a little door on the side, and Peter parked next to them. He didn't get out right away, though, just sat in his car, looking up. It was like looking up the edge of a serrated blade, he thought unhappily. Just walking up them was going to rip him apart so badly, he wouldn't even feel the pain until he was halfway home.

He had to, he thought. He had to. He owed them this. Both of them. Bodi and Michael, he owed them.

THE first time Peter actually saw Bodi Kovacs, he and Michael were at church. Peter hated church. He hated wearing a dress shirt and a tie, he hated peeling the lint and the dust off his good slacks, and he hated the way Michael's hand-me-down shoes pinched his feet. He hated all the blood and the gore coming in from the stained glass windows in sunlit splendor. He *really* hated the way the preacher—and they went through a lot of them because Daisy was so small it was barely a political blip on an ambitious young preacher's map—was always determined to convince Daisy that he held the key to keeping them all out of hell. But the way he railed at everyone from fornicators to liberals to doctors to homosexuals made Peter wonder how empty it really was going to be in heaven if any of the people sitting wide-eyed in the pews got there. Peter had seen a little more of the world than most of Daisy. He wasn't sure if they knew how short a list of people the preacher was really leaving for heaven. He was, however, pretty sure that a lot of the people in those pews who thought they were going wouldn't be on that list.

So there they were, looking dispiritedly at the long-assed Bible verse the preacher was reading at them, when Michael got a tap on the shoulder from the kid sitting behind him. Michael turned around for a second, and then, surreptitiously, slid two drawings (made in pen on the white part of the service programs) in front of the Bible for Peter to see. One of them was of Michael in a Superman outfit, and the other was of Peter dressed as Batman.

Peter risked a glance over his shoulder and saw a pair of blue eyes, pale in color and slightly crossed, and longish sandy-blond hair. He also saw a tentative smile, and he found himself smiling back, and just at that minute, he thought that maybe he could forgive Bodi Kovacs for being the new center of Michael's world.

That was Peter's first actual look at Bodi but not the first time Peter had heard about him. Bodi moved to town in Michael's junior year, and until that moment in church, Peter was wildly, ferociously jealous.

Peter had lived in Daisy for around a year before Bodi showed up, and in that year Michael had been the most wonderful thing in his life. Ever. Peter's mother had taken them from apartment to apartment, from school to school, as she'd struggled to keep the two of them fed and housed on minimum-wage jobs. She managed to keep them mostly fed, but their home was never anyplace permanent. So waking up in the same bed for a year, that had been something new for Peter, and not entirely unwelcome in spite of the fact that she'd had to leave him to make that happen.

Michael, though. He was so much better than waking up in the same bed. Michael was happy when he woke up and came down the stairs. There were always Cheerios in the cupboard for breakfast, but Michael always tried to do better. Michael could make pancakes or sneak mini marshmallows out of the cupboard to put on the Cheerios to make them better. Michael took Peter to the quiet places to fish and showed him how to check out books from the library. Michael was on the football team, and when Peter was in the stands, Michael waved to him from the field. He was on the track team, and he dared Peter to run with him, and Peter did—not fast, but he could last longer, and Michael said it made him a better runner to just keep going.

Aunt Aileen gave Peter the bed and let him eat at her table. She bought him clothes—two pairs of jeans, five shirts—for the school year, and gave him a toy or a book at Christmas. Yes, Aunt Aileen took care of him, but Michael gave him a home.

So when Michael and Bodi started hanging out together, Peter was devastated.

"You're going running with him?" he asked the same Sunday that Bodi drew a picture of him as Batman.

"Yeah—you want to come?"

"No. You'll probably just go faster than me anyway." Even though Peter loved that picture and put it immediately in his favorite book about astronomy to keep it safe, he was also very aware that the only place he could be Batman was in ink. Batman was brave, and Peter tried to be, because he promised his mother, but he could really only be brave about one thing, and that was just being who he was. Bodi had a lithe, rangy body—he could probably run much faster than Peter—and Michael was the darling of the track team. The two older boys would go much faster than Peter, he just knew it.

But Bodi trotted up the porch steps wearing old basketball shorts instead of running shorts and an overlarge T-shirt instead of a tank top. Peter's initial impression of him still held—longish sandy-blond hair, streaking yellow in the summer sun, and crossed blue eyes, with one of those faces where the cheekbones stood out and the cheeks hollowed in. When he was looking somewhere else, he looked fierce and, especially with the long hair, a little bit scary, but he'd smiled at Peter with sort of a quiet grace.

"You comin'?" he asked, like there wasn't any doubt, and Peter found himself nodding.

"I'm slow," he confessed, his voice suddenly gravelly as he stared committedly at his shoes with their separating rubber.

"We're just running to the swimming hole, right?" Bodi asked, and Michael closed his eyes.

"That was supposed to be a surprise, genius!"

Peter perked up. "Yeah?" Michael had taken him for much of the summer, but there were bigger kids there, high school students and some of the kids from junior high who had not yet made Peter's life a long misery. (He saw it coming, but he hadn't yet been fished out of a garbage can. Not yet.) So Peter loved the swimming hole, but no—he didn't want to go alone.

"Yeah," Bodi said, smiling that unconscious, not-quite-there smile. "The swimming hole. Let's go become one with nature."

Michael rolled his eyes. "God, Bodi, you are so weird."

15

Suddenly Bodi's smile clicked into an intense focus—and all that focus was on Michael's face. "You like me that way, right?"

Michael laughed and socked him in the arm. "It's why we hang out," he confirmed. "C'mon, Petey. It's gonna be fuckin' hot!"

Peter's eyes got big. "Michael, don't swear when she can hear you."

Michael hunched his shoulders. "Crap," he muttered. "Yeah, yeah—if we're not careful I'll be listening to why I'm going to hell instead of going swimming. Go grab a couple of towels, okay? Let's get the hell out of here."

Peter did, and the two-mile run to the swimming hole left them a big sweaty mess. No one else was there when they arrived—and they wouldn't be, either. Peter and Michael knew for a fact that there was a church dance that night, and most of the other kids were setting up for it. But Michael and Peter weren't in the youth group—in spite of Aileen's pleading—and they had the tree-shaded ravine to themselves. They got there, and Michael and Peter tore off their shirts and their shoes and socks and turned around and—

Bodi was naked. He wasn't looking at them. Instead, he was climbing up on the jumping rock without any self-consciousness at all. Peter's mouth went dry. Bodi was naked, and he had hair—golden-brown hair down there—and his privates swung, heavy and uncut, practically thudding against his thighs as he moved. He was skinny because he was barely fourteen, but the muscles in his thighs and ass were heavy and defined, and the muscles in his stomach and his chest were cut enough to flex as he climbed. He was beautiful and graceful and completely unaware that skinny-dipping wasn't what you did in the swimming hole.

Peter and Michael both blinked, and Peter was about to open his mouth to say *You can't do that!* when Michael turned to him and winked.

And shucked his shorts too.

"But what if someone comes!" Peter hissed, and Michael grinned.

"Well, then we'll all be naked, and no one will make a thing out of it, like he's weird or anything," Michael whispered back.

"It *is* weird!" Peter told him, staring, and Michael scowled at him.

"Not for him!" There was something wistful in Michael's voice, something admiring, and for a moment, they watched Bodi, standing in the sun, his hair shining and his tanned back sweaty and shining too. He turned toward them and gave that easy copacetic grin, and something in Peter's chest hurt. He swallowed.

"I don't want to be naked," he whispered painfully. "My thing ain't shaped like his."

Michael looked at him and nodded, both of them sharing a faintly scandalized moment. "Nobody's is," Michael muttered. "Nobody at school, anyway." Then he smiled a little dreamily. "I think it's kind of neat." He looked at Peter. "I sort of want to touch it."

Peter looked back at him, stricken and embarrassed, and he was on the verge of confessing that yes, yes, he wanted to touch it too, more than anything, when Bodi called to them both and then ran off the edge of the rock and whooped as he fell toward the river. Both boys watched as his arms and legs flailed in the air, and then Michael, naked and happy, went running for the rock.

Peter left his trunks on. He was eleven, and his thing was small and he didn't have any hair and he didn't want to draw comparisons. But that night, he remembered Bodi, tan and lean and beautiful, swimming in the cool of deep water, oblivious to his beauty or his uniqueness in the singular, faceless choir of Daisy.

They swam that day and Bodi pointed out things like the shape of the leaves or the brutality of the cloudless blue sky. He talked about the ocean and of this Byron poem he'd read. At one point Bodi and Peter treaded water and watched as Michael—fearless and naked, just like Bodi—leapt off the rock and flipped in midair like a diving champion, and Bodi actually recited most of the poem. And he liked to take care of people. One minute he'd be talking about

17

everything from Romantic poets to lamias, and the next he'd be telling Peter very seriously to get out of the cold water because his lips were turning blue.

And then he'd be wrestling with Michael and laughing openly, contagiously, with a sound almost like a seal barking interspersed with big belly-spawned jackass brays. Peter lost some of his shyness at this point and tried to tickle him while Michael wrapped his legs around Bodi's waist in the water and held him down—just so they could hear that infectious, amazing sound.

Peter fell asleep that night and dreamed of Bodi, that lean face so close it was blocking the sun, his hair a shiny satin curtain letting light through. Bodi leaned closer to Peter, closer and closer, until Peter could smell the sweat and river water on his skin and feel the warmth of his breath. Closer until they were almost touching.

Peter woke up soaked in sweat, smelling semen on his sheets for the first time. He'd had health class; he knew what just happened. He'd told his mother before she'd brought him to his Aunt Aileen's that he thought boys were more beautiful than girls, and she'd told him that he would have to be either brave or quiet about that, especially in Daisy. He'd told her he'd be brave, but he'd been thinking about changing his mind. Maybe two days before that trip to the swimming hole, he would have chosen to be quiet about who he wanted to kiss. Since his mother had brought him to Daisy, he'd had to live through those stifling sermons in the church, where liking boys had been given an unholy name, and school was already difficult and uncomfortable for someone who knew more about the world than the rest of the kids. Two days before he saw Bodi Kovacs naked and beautiful and laughing, maybe he would have told the quiet lie. He would have told himself he'd ejaculated in his sleep because Bodi was pretty as a girl, even though his lean cheeks and cheekbones were all masculine, in spite of the full mouth. He would have sided with Aunt Aileen and said that Bodi was just too damned weird to hang with, and he would have found reasons to dodge his company, even if it meant missing out on his cousin's company as well.

But he'd seen that look on Michael's face, that look of dreamy wonder as Bodi had climbed the rock under the sun. Michael could do no wrong. If Michael could look at Bodi like that, so could Peter.

Peter started looking forward to seeing Bodi after school in Michael's company. And he started washing his own sheets.

PETER stood in front of the door and listened for a moment to the sounds of Pearl Jam thrumming softly through the door. He could smell pot smoke, and he sighed. Yeah, Bodi had liked to do that before he left town; there was no reason to think he'd stopped. But then, Bodi had needed it sometimes. When Bodi was actually paying attention, the world was too abrasive for him to survive in it.

Peter knocked loud and hard, in case Bodi had fallen asleep, and was happy when he heard footsteps padding across a carpeted floor. The light from the peephole dimmed, and then there was a fumbling at the door handle.

"Oh God! Peter!"

The door swung open, and there was Bodi.

He looked like he'd showered—his hair was wet, and the smell of shampoo still lingered over the smell of smoke and of the beer he'd obviously been drinking. His face was even leaner at twenty-six than it had been at fifteen, and his hair fell to his shoulders, layered at his face like it was still the seventies and he was listening to old Boston instead of new Pearl Jam. His eyes were bloodshot and shadowed, but the smile he gave Peter was still sweet.

"Petey! Brother—what's up?"

He gave that hand-clasp/hug thing, something Peter had only ever done with Bodi and Michael, except that when they went in to touch chests, Bodi got closer, leaned closer than he ever had before. It was like he was seeking warmth.

"Hey, Bodi," Peter said quietly, thinking that he moved like someone who hadn't been touched in a long time. "Can I come in?"

Bodi nodded and ignored the stash, even though Peter had never approved. They went into what was a neat little apartment space, open plan, with a sofa facing a plasma television against the back wall. There was a counter behind it opening into a small kitchen. Beyond that was a tiny hall space with what Peter guessed would be a bedroom, a bathroom, and probably a closet. To the side there was a bookshelf with old, dog-eared copies of Byron and Keats, as well as some new paperbacks. They'd been read again and again and again until the spines were broken and the titles almost indecipherable, which didn't surprise Peter. Bodi might love classic poetry, but Peter had long ago figured out that the reading of it didn't come easy to him.

Beyond the bookshelves, the floors were hardwood, the walls were paneled, and the throw rug under the couch was a cream color, and plush. There were a few stains on the rug—it had been lived on—but it was generally in good condition, and the couch was sort of a soft, kidskin leather. There was a canvas on an easel in the breakfast nook where usually a table would be, which meant the pictures on the walls had probably been painted by Bodi himself—wildflowers, the ocean, a lighthouse, all of them in bright, joyous, intense pastels.

Yeah. The heart of the boy Peter had known still lived here.

"What's up?" Bodi asked again. "Man, what's it been—two years?"

"Six," Peter said, his throat rough, wondering why Bodi would think two. Six years. Six years ago Michael had enlisted in the army and left Daisy, California, without a backward glance—or at least that's what Peter thought until Bodi spoke again.

"Yeah, I forget. You know, Michael came back two years ago—on leave." He looked sort of despondently at the stash and the beer on his coffee table. "It's like time stopped."

"He came back?" Peter asked, his heart whooshing in his ears. "He… he told Aunt Aileen he was staying in Europe between tours!"

Bodi looked away and moved restlessly toward the kitchen counter. He was skinny—God, almost as skinny as when he was fourteen—and that joyful movement, that movement that was proud and unafraid, that was gone. His shoulders drooped, and he slouched, like he was trying not to catch the world's attention. Well, the world had been pretty fucking awful to Bodi; Peter didn't blame him for wanting to disappear.

"Yeah?" Bodi said, sounding honestly surprised. He sighed and turned, then started rooting in the refrigerator. "Well. I'm sorry. I didn't know that. Look, little brother, can I get you something? I... you know, I fucking missed you, right? Just because me and Michael ain't... you know... friends no more, doesn't mean...."

Peter swallowed and tried to get past a betrayal he'd never known about. "Bodi," he said softly, "I think you need to sit down."

Bodi straightened and closed the refrigerator door and swallowed. "No," he said, his voice suddenly strong and assertive like it had been when Peter had tried to thank him for beating up bullies. *No, little brother. Don't thank me. That's what we do for each other, right?*

"No what?" Peter looked around at the full ashtray and the table cluttered with beer bottles and wondered how much Bodi had drunk that night. How much had he smoked? *Oh, God, Bodi—have you been living on beer and pot for two years?*

"No," Bodi said, leaning his head on the refrigerator. "You're not going to come here after six... after six *goddamned years*, when you knew where the fuck I was, and you got to stay in your sweet little home and have a fucking future, and you're not going to come tell me that."

"You think I got a future?" Peter snapped. "Bodi, I pay *rent*, for Christ's sake, in a house where the only other inhabitant fucking *hates* me."

Bodi looked at him, squinting through the big thing, the big awful red thing they were both trying to ignore. "That bitch makes you pay rent?"

21

"Yeah!" Peter half laughed.

"But you were supposed to be goin' to school! Michael, he says he's been sending you money for school, dammit!"

Peter's mouth fell open.

Fuck. Oh fuck. His chest froze, and he couldn't breathe.

"He sent postcards," Peter managed. "He sent postcards, just saying hi. Not even letters, like the ones I wrote back. But I've been saving on my own. I... every cent I've got—I've got three years' tuition saved."

"Fuck," Bodi muttered. "You weren't supposed to do that. That's—goddammit, that's... he told me he was sending you money. What happened to it?"

Oh yeah. They could both guess.

"Fucking church," Peter whispered. "Goddamned fucking church. I hope they liked my goddamned college experience, motherfuckers. 'Cause I'm gonna go anyway."

Yeah, Aileen would do that, wouldn't she? Give money Michael had earmarked for Peter to the church? To apologize for the two of them. A couple of abominations under her roof.

Peter took a deep breath against another unexpected betrayal. It was the day for them, maybe. Great. Now he had to be the one to betray, because that's what it felt like, giving news like this.

"Bodi," he whispered, "that sucks. And it's gonna hit me later. But man... man, you gotta sit down, and you gotta let me tell you."

"No," Bodi whispered again. "Please, Petey. God. It was bad enough when he left that second time. Don't fucking break my heart."

"I'm sorry, Bodi. He's dead. The service is in a week."

Bodi's voice wobbled when he spoke next, and, goddammit, he was still leaning his head against the refrigerator. "His bike."

"What?"

22

"Where's his fuckin' bike, Petey? He had... he left... oh fuck. He left me high and dry, but he left instructions for that fuckin' bike."

"I sold mine. I haven't ridden since I was sixteen," Peter said numbly, thinking about the *other* bike, the big Harley, broken and twisted and collecting dust in the garage next to Aileen's white Dodge Caravan.

"He doesn't want you to ride," Bodi said, and Peter wondered if he would ever use the past tense. "He's never wanted you to. He... God, Peter. He had plans for you, you know that? Three years' tuition? Why the fuck are you still living there?"

Peter swallowed. "Because my only family still lives there," he said roughly. Then, because he had to: "Lived."

"He ain't lived there for six years."

Peter wished Bodi would turn around. Wished he'd let Peter in. Wished he'd cry, wished he'd rage or lapse into poetry or anything, just fucking anything, just fucking *grieve, Bodi, grieve! This feeling's gonna make you sick, sick to die, if you don't just fucking let it go!*

"She makes up his bed every month," Peter said, his throat aching. "His motorcycle's there. He...." *My cousin Michael loves me, and I live with him.* Oh fuck.

Bodi turned around, and his face was like an axe blade, and nothing, not a sigh or a tear or a softening of the lines around his mouth, was going to escape without drawing blood.

"Well then we'll do that thing he wanted, and that'll let you go. It'll free you, 'kay, Petey? Me'n Michael, we can set you free."

Peter wanted to hold him so damned bad. *The only thing that will set me free, Bodi, is taking care of you.*

"What do I have to do?" he asked, because it was the only thing he had to give Bodi that Bodi would take right now.

"Dust it off. Fix it up, polish it, get it running. I'll be there... God. Not tomorrow." Bodi closed his eyes and pushed his palms against them and groaned. "I'll be there the day after. Got shit to do, orders to finish. Can't close up the shop or I won't pay my rent... fuck... why do I always forget about shit like that?" He pulled his palms away and looked at Peter with a hard face, almost a soldier's face. "I'll be there in two days, okay? I guess I could ask my mom to put me up, but I don't think *that'll* happen. I'll bring camping shit, sleep up by the river. If you can sneak me in for a shower or something, I can maybe stay until the funeral. Maybe not. Either way, I got to leave that day." Most of this sounded like he was talking to himself, like he was making plans in his head, so that way he'd remember them when it came time to carry them out. It's what he'd always done.

"I'll go home and fix a snack, right? And feed Juliet, and read to her. Okay. Good. Then I can do my homework and have dinner for Mom when she gets home. I can do that."

"Who you talking to, Bodi?" Peter asked curiously from the backseat of Michael's mom's car as they drove home after Bodi and Michael's football practice. Peter did his homework while he waited, but he always loved to watch them play.

"Himself," Michael said softly. "Sh... just let him do that. He gets it straight in his head, and then he doesn't worry about it anymore."

"Okay," Bodi said now, "that sounds like a plan."

"Yeah," Peter murmured. "That's a plan."

Bodi looked at him unhappily. "You got to stay the night, Petey. It's, like, midnight."

Peter shook his head, although he *longed* to sleep on the couch and make sure Bodi had breakfast and got to work okay. "I've got to get back," he said through a thick throat. "I promised—"

"Who, her?" Bodi's lip curled with derision. "No. Fuck that. I'll fuckin' tackle you for your goddamned keys, little brother. It's dark, and that road's fucking murder, and I... God. I just don't need the idea of you out there tonight, right?"

Peter swallowed and, for a moment, weighed what he'd thought he owed his Aunt Aileen with what he owed Michael, owed Bodi, and then the scale broke. "Yeah," he said softly. "Get me a pillow, a blanket. I'll call and tell them I won't be back tonight."

Bodi nodded and disappeared for a moment, and Peter pulled out his cell phone and dialed the wall phone Aileen still had up in her bright gold kitchen.

"Joelle? Yeah. I'll be back the day after tomorrow, 'bout noon."

There was a startled squawk. "Two days? You were only supposed to be gone—"

"Yeah, I'm sorry."

"Sorry is a piss-poor excuse for family, Peter."

Peter winced when the woman's voice got acerbic. "Yeah, well, Bodi needs somebody too, and you fuckers 'bout stripped him of everyone, so I'm staying here."

"After all that woman has done for you—"

"Ask her where my college money is, Joelle, and then get back to me on that."

He hit End Call and took a deep breath. Bodi was setting out bedding, lots of it, which was good, because you could hear the rush of the sea from here, and the fog was rolling in. It could chill you to the bone if you weren't careful, even in the late spring. Peter moved forward and helped Bodi tuck in the sheet and lay down the blanket. Bodi's hands were battered from working on the bikes, but even when they'd been kids, he'd spent hours scrubbing to get a lot of the engine grease out. Back then, Peter liked looking at them, with their short-trimmed nails, and wondering what they'd feel like on his skin. Even now, even after so long, Bodi made him want things he'd never had a chance to have.

Bodi looked down at his hands and suddenly reached out and grabbed Peter's, turning it over and tracing the thick scar across the palm.

"God," he murmured, "I remember when you got that. Michael was gonna shit his pants."

Peter looked at it too. Remembered wondering when it would hurt. Realized he felt like that now.

"Just me," Peter said quietly. "I'm still a clumsy little shit."

It was true too—although now he was tall, even taller than Bodi, and still scrawny. Bodi used to have a wide chest, and it had seemed perfect, the perfect thing to block out the scary world. Now Peter wished he could fold over the man, protect him that way, because no one had ever blocked out the scary world for Bodi.

"Yeah?" Bodi asked, not seeming to notice that he was stroking Peter's palm softly with a callused finger.

"Yeah," Peter said quietly and clasped Bodi's hand.

Bodi looked up and met Peter's eyes and then closed his own against whatever he saw in Peter's face. "I was going to come visit," he said quietly. "'Bout two years ago. Then Michael came home on leave."

He dropped Peter's hand and walked away, stopping at the hallway for a moment. "Bathroom's on your left, more blankets on the right, there's an extra toothbrush in the sink. Good night, little brother."

Peter sighed. "Bodi!" he called back, wanting something, some acknowledgement that Michael was dead, some explanation for the shivers that were racking his body that had nothing to do with Michael and everything to do with his hand in Bodi's for a solid minute, with that absently stroking finger.

"What?" Bodi turned around and blinked.

"Why—" Peter swallowed, unable to fuck him up any more. "Why were you going to come to visit?"

Bodi shrugged. "I loved you too, little brother. You knew that."

And then he disappeared in the bedroom. Peter stripped down to his T-shirt and briefs, then slid into his makeshift bed and wished bitterly that "I loved you too" was what it sounded like. It was the only thing Peter had ever wanted and the one thing he'd never dared to ask for. Just hearing the words gave him hope, and hope hurt too goddamned much tonight.

HOME MAKING

BODI stood over him, tracing his cheekbone with a long finger, and Peter tilted his face up to let it happen. He reached up, wanting to return the touch, and Bodi closed his eyes.

"You'd only leave me too, little brother. I can't live through that again."

PETER awakened with a start, the gray of the dawn barely creeping through the heavy drapes on the window. Every window this close to the ocean had heavy drapes—you needed the insulation, or you'd never get warm some days.

Bodi slept on, and Peter sat up quickly to pull on his jeans and tennis shoes and unfashionable windbreaker. Normally he wouldn't risk being seen before he'd combed his hair or brushed his teeth, but his imperative to take care of Bodi overwhelmed even *his* geekish sense of propriety. He left a note on his folded blankets saying *I'll be back.* He couldn't bear that Bodi would think he'd left, even for a short trip to the store.

The bored, tired clerk in the little grocery store didn't even look at him twice as he ran in and came out with some eggs, some milk and juice, bread, butter, sausage, and sandwich fixings in the bag. He also bought tea, the fragrant, tangy herbal kind with rose hip and lemon in it, because that was probably the one thing he'd taken away from Aunt Aileen that he didn't regret or resent.

He came back quietly, thankful that people in this neck of the woods made it a habit not to lock their doors so he didn't have to feel guilty for leaving it open for half an hour, and started breakfast.

By the time Bodi stumbled out of bed an hour later, the kitchen was clean. The beer bottles thrown outside in the recycler, the ashtray emptied outside and washed, and the stash... well, it was flushed down the toilet, but Peter didn't want to tell Bodi that immediately. As soon as Peter heard Bodi rolling out of bed and taking his morning piss, Peter started the coffee and popped the toast in, thrilled that the guy had a toaster, actually, even if it had needed a thorough wiping off and the tray underneath had needed to be scrubbed with the abrasive part of the sponge.

"Oh God... Peter?" He was wearing sweats on the bottom and nothing on the top, even though his skin was raised and puckered in the ocean-morning chill.

"Hey," Peter said, smiling tentatively. "Good morning."

Bodi squinted. "Oh geez—breakfast?"

"Yeah, I bought some groceries and shit so you'd have something when you got home too."

Bodi just stood there, blinking through bloodshot eyes. "Why'd you do that?"

"Because somebody should be."

Bodi stopped and scowled. "So where have you been for the last six years?" His voice held real venom, and Peter swallowed and stirred the eggs so the sausage scramble wouldn't burn.

"Feeling hella guilty," Peter whispered through gravel. "I didn't even know how to follow you six years ago."

Some of Bodi's anger seemed to have evaporated when he spoke. "You were sixteen."

"Fifteen," Peter muttered. "'Cause if I was sixteen, I would have had my own fucking driver's license and...." He shuddered and sighed.

"Yeah," Bodi muttered. "There was so much fucked up about that day, I don't even know where you'd start."

"Tragedies are like that," Peter said gently, and Bodi grimaced.

"Tragedies involve heroes with a fatal flaw, Petey. Who's got the fucking flaw?"

"I do," Peter said, because he'd had six years to think about it. He dished up the eggs like his entire body wasn't sweating and his stomach wasn't roiling from having this conversation. "I've been coming to Arcata for years, but I didn't come see you. I was the one who had the power. That day, I was the one who—"

"Don't finish that sentence." Bodi was standing up straight now, his eyes focusing almost meditatively somewhere beyond Peter's head. For a moment he was the beautiful boy on the rock and his serenity was unblemished. "You didn't do anything wrong."

"Neither did you or Michael." Peter knew that in the depths of his soul.

"Yeah," Bodi said, suddenly fixing those almost crossed blue eyes on Peter's face. "But you wouldn't know it by where we are now."

"You're still here," Peter said with determination. "And now so am I. Eat something, for Christ's sake. I thought pot was supposed to give you the fucking munchies, Bodi."

Bodi raised his eyebrows. "Geez, little brother, for a moment there you sounded like your aunt Aileen."

Peter clamped down on the edginess in his voice. "Don't get nasty, Bodi—I remembered ketchup."

Bodi never could hold a grudge or an evil mood. Apparently not even now, when he'd had his heart broken until it almost wasn't even Bodi's anymore. He sat at the counter and reached out a bare arm, and Peter handed him a plate. Bodi set it down in front of him while Peter's own heart broke one more time.

"Jesus," he whispered. "Bodi."

Bodi looked up at him and then down at the crook of his right arm, where little neat puncture scars that lined his vein were clearly visible on the pale skin. He shrugged, although Peter watched his throat flush and blotch, and the inside of his arms too—except the scars, of course.

30

"They're old," he said quietly. "Clean from the hard shit for almost—"

"Two years," Peter said, not sure he could actually see through the spots swimming in his vision. "God, Bodi, what'd he do to you?"

Bodi took a bite of eggs and chewed blindly without appearing to taste. "It wasn't on purpose, little brother," he said with resignation. "He... God. We all hurt, didn't we?"

Peter swallowed. Bodi. Michael had left Peter—it was inevitable, right? Big brother moves out of the house; little brother has to wait his turn. But... oh God....

"Bodi, how could he leave you?"

Bodi looked up from his eggs—he'd actually slowed down and had seemed to enjoy them in the silence, but now he dropped his fork on his plate like that little portion was all he wanted. "You really think Michael died yesterday, don't you, Peter? You really think that's true."

"Three days ago. That's what the telegram said."

Bodi nodded and crammed a bite of toast in his mouth like someone was holding a gun to his head. "That's cause you're young," he said with his mouthful. He swallowed again and took another bite.

"What do you mean?"

"You worshipped the guy," Bodi said, still eating like he had to. "We all did."

"And?"

Bodi shoveled one more bite into his mouth and swallowed hard, and it looked like he might need a broom handle and a gorilla to get it down.

Bodi shoved his plate sideways and rested his chin on his hands.

"He came here out of the blue after four years. Four years I'd been building my life back, right? You remember that. I showed up here and got a job when I thought *no* one would hire me, remembered to go to work, managed to pay rent. It wasn't supposed to be just me. It was supposed to be both of us... and suddenly I'm sneaking my shit out of my mom's garage in the middle of the night and Michael's helping me and finding that shitty apartment that got torn down two years ago and... and he didn't say anything to me, you hear? You may have known about the military, but—"

"We didn't," Peter said through a dry throat. "He didn't tell us he'd enlisted. He left a letter on my end table, the keys to the fuckin' bike and his car, and caught a bus out of town."

Bodi swallowed. "Yeah? You got a letter?"

Peter nodded and took the plate down and put it in the sink. "Did you?"

"Yeah. It was his orders and the last line of a Springsteen song, the fucker."

"Bobby Jean?"

"I miss you, baby," Bodi quoted, and Peter joined him, because he got the same fucking letter. "Good luck, good-bye, Bobby Jean."

"Fucker," Peter echoed.

"I didn't know he'd done that to you too," Bodi said quietly.

"You had other things on your mind," Peter told him and swallowed hard against the unfairness of it all. He paused, because there were echoes upon echoes here of the one thing no one had talked about, not even six years ago, when it had just happened. No, everyone had been so eager to pin blame on Bodi and Michael that they'd never really thought about the other victim of that horrible day. "Bodi?" Peter asked. There was a pause long enough for him to wash the next dish and stack it. "Have I ever told you how sorry I am? About Juliet, I mean? I...." He stopped then, because Bodi was looking at him, stunned. "Bodi?"

Bodi shook his head. "Where's the pot?" he asked, and Peter winced.

32

"Not here."

"No screwing around here. Where's the fucking pot?"

"I dumped it down the toilet and threw the box away." Peter stared at him with determination. Bodi needed keeping, and that box of stash had been allowed to stay in this little apartment way too long.

"Why'd you do that?" Bodi asked almost desperately. "Jesus, Peter, what'd I ever do to you?"

"You broke my heart, you stupid bastard, now tell me why that one thing sends you into such a fuckin' tailspin, dammit!"

"You threw it away?" Bodi turned around and, with lost eyes, took in the clean, dusted state of his living room. "Why?"

Peter stalked around the kitchen and put his hands on Bodi's shoulders, shaking them hard. "Dammit, Bodi—I just said I was sorry about her. Why's that gotta send you screaming for—"

"Because!" Bodi shouted, and then his voice dropped and he closed his eyes tight. "Because," he said now, his voice almost too low to hear. "God, Peter, six years. No one's said that to me. Not even Michael."

Peter pulled Bodi close against his chest and buried his nose in Bodi's long, sleep-tangled hair. "I'm sorry," he said. Everything hurt, even his skin.

Bodi pushed away. "I gotta go take a shower," he muttered. "I'm totally rank." He wasn't. His hair had been wet and his face soft from a shower the night before, and he smelled like sleep, but not sweat, but Peter let him go. Suddenly he hated himself, hated the *world*, too much to follow him, to make him talk. To make it right.

PETER was thirteen the first time Bodi and Michael missed church. His first reaction was relief—for them, of course. Church was an onerous, screaming and hollering affair of people moaning and calling "Amen" and "Hallelujah," and the pastor—whoever it was—

thundering on about shit that Peter was starting to think preachers knew nothing about.

Faith in God? Yeah, Peter had heard of it. God hadn't stepped up to be Peter's father, and he certainly hadn't ponied up to help out Peter's mother when she'd been working her ass off. Yeah, most of the town told him God was behind Peter's aunt Aileen taking Peter in, but then, nothing made you sick of a fact quicker than having your face rubbed in it until your nose was raw. As far as Peter was concerned, God poured salt on the wound and egged the bullies on, and he hadn't seen a damned thing to change his mind.

So Michael and Bodi disappeared one Sunday, and Peter cheered them on—and then, just as suddenly, was wounded to his vitals.

They'd left him behind.

Peter went *everywhere* with them. He sat on the bench for their football games, sat in the car as they drove around after practice. He and Michael took turns, one of them keeping Bodi company while he watched his sister, the other one doing chores at home, so Bodi didn't have to be alone in those long hours after he told the babysitter to go home.

Being with Bodi's sister was difficult enough anyway.

Juliet had tripped and fallen when she was a baby—a long fall down a set of stairs—and she'd smashed her forehead on a brick hearth below. The results had been... unpredictable at best. Diagnosed with frontal lobe damage, Juliet was moody, angry, bright, articulate, and impulsive in the most dangerous of ways. Some days she would sit, working out trigonometry problems with an almost frightening intensity. Her concentration was so singular that one winter afternoon after Peter had tripped on a potted plant and knocked it into the fireplace, barely escaping setting Bodi's mom's house on fire, Juliet's only reaction had been to wipe her eyes from the smoke.

Some days she would watch cartoons and giggle like an eight-year-old. She was Peter's age, and she could do grown-up math, but she never seemed to act like a kid his age, and certainly not on the cartoon days, when she acted much younger. Peter liked those days—he could handle watching cartoons and laughing and rehashing the plots, because that was easy, and he didn't have to risk making Juliet angry.

Bodi still had a scar on his shoulder from when she was eight. He'd told her to please leave his picture book alone, and when he'd come back from the bathroom, he'd found her hacking it up with a steak knife. He'd tried to stop her and had ended up with a three-inch puncture wound by his neck. Their mother had locked up the knives, forks, screwdrivers, breakable china, lighters, extension cords, rat poison, toasters, and sports equipment after that, but even as Juliet had grown, the instruction had been implicit: she was not to be left alone under any circumstances.

Bodi was terrified he'd fuck up his watch. When football practice or track practice ended, he'd begin to get nervous. He'd start his list in his head and repeat it again and again until he'd remembered everything, from Juliet's snack to the order in which he'd do his homework to what he planned to do for himself when his mother came home from work. Sometimes, he'd get to work on that motorcycle or read the book he'd checked out, but sometimes, he'd watch his sister some more while his mother watched television or simply recovered from the stress of her own day.

In the daytime, her medical insurance paid for Juliet's supervision. On Sundays, it was the church.

"God, Peter," Michael had said before they'd started missing services, "I think sometimes the only reason he goes is so he doesn't have to worry."

Peter had sat in Bodi's room sometimes when he'd been there to keep Bodi company. Bodi had installed his own locks on the inside of his door, and after the third time he and his mother had found Juliet wandering around the riverbank near the rapids, about two miles from the main drag, he'd installed one on the outside of hers. It was the only way he knew how to sleep.

And in spite of that, Peter knew Bodi loved his sister. He saved jokes for her—the simple ones that third graders got.

"Hey, Juliet—why did the chicken cross the road?"

"Why?"

"Because it was stapled to the turkey!"

Her laugh—God. That's why Bodi loved her. It was... free. Juliet didn't worry about having a supervisor. She didn't worry about what she said to people or how it would make them feel. It was difficult to deal with, and it made Bodi both too young and too old at the same time, but God—if there was a God—that laugh might have been proof that he existed.

"Who's that?" she'd ask when Peter took his turn with Bodi.

"That's Michael's cousin, Peter."

"He looks like a prick."

"Juliet, he's very nice."

"He's uptight and scared. Do I scare you, dumbshit?"

It took Peter a month or two to figure out the answer to this. "What did the vampire say to the ghost?"

"I don't know, what?"

"Don't try to trick me, I can see right through you!"

And then she'd laugh, and Bodi would look at Peter like he'd solved world hunger or something.

But it was exhausting. Bodi and Peter would try to take her through her schoolwork, and she was capable—she was fully capable of doing Peter's work—but God help her if she got frustrated. She'd once thrown Peter's own math book at him so hard it had given him a nosebleed, and he'd had to pay to replace the book. He and Michael had pooled their allowances, because the Good Lord forbid they asked Aunt Aileen for that money. She'd have to know why, and she and the rest of the town were of the opinion that the girl was cursed for some reason—the preacher liked to say that God didn't visit his wrath down upon children for nothing, right?

And it made Peter sick. He'd done his research; he'd asked Bodi questions. Bodi wasn't stupid. He'd done his research too. She'd fallen. She'd hurt herself. Some hurts didn't get fixed. It wasn't God and it wasn't wrath, it was just a bunch of teenagers trying to take care of a big, strong girl who was totally capable of hurting them if they gave her half a chance.

So Peter didn't begrudge Bodi and Michael slipping off into the bright afternoons, but damned if he didn't want to go with them.

So the next Sunday, he parked his bike between the big oak tree and the church, where no one would see it until the social afterward. He climbed the tree and watched as the two of them simply lingered behind pretty much half the town as they walked through the big, creaky vaulted oak doors. As the last of the elderly were being assisted into the vestry, Bodi and Michael simply slipped away.

Peter waited until the usher closed the big double doors and then hopped on his bike and followed them.

He almost despaired when he heard Bodi's motorcycle start up a few blocks north of the church, but then he realized that if that's where they were starting the motorcycle up (probably so no one would hear it in the church and look for the two of them), there was only one place they'd be going.

Sure enough, he saw the motorcycle parked as he pumped his bike up the mountain to the turnoff where you parked to visit the swimming hole.

He dropped his bike next to the cycle and went walking down between the guardrails and sliding down the embankment to the more even forest floor. He was looking forward to swimming with the two of them, when he heard something odd that made him stop, slow down… sneak.

It was the sound Michael made when he was eating cake or cookies, except lower, more urgent, and he was making it a lot and louder as Peter got near.

Peter knew about the stand of scrub brush that stood between two aspen trees, and he crept behind that and sat quietly, listening to Michael... moan.

And then he heard Bodi's quiet laughter.

And he knew. His cock (not his "thing" anymore, he was old enough now to call it his cock) was hard and it hurt and his shoulders shook with tension before he turned around and looked through the foliage to the bare little shaded meadow with the granite jumping rock behind it.

They were on a sleeping bag, one that Peter recognized from the garage, even though it wasn't used for camping that often.

They were both as naked as that first day they'd all gone swimming together. Bodi's body, tan, lean, filling out in the shoulders, was moving over Michael's, and Peter watched as they kissed, even as Bodi's back and hips undulated and he pushed himself up against Michael and Michael arched against him. They bucked for a moment, and then Michael made a whine in his throat, a "pretty, pretty please!" sound, and Bodi pulled back and chuckled.

"I've been wanting to try this," he said, and then he kissed Michael's chin, and his neck, and down.... He stopped at the nipples, and Peter watched, fascinated, as he spent some time there, doing fiddly, indulgent things, but not for long.

Michael snapped, "God, Bodi, you're fuckin' killing me!"

Bodi laughed softly and moved the hand on Michael's nipple down to his erect cock. He must have squeezed then, because Michael said, "Harder. Like this!" and wrapped his fingers around Bodi's. They both stroked him together, and Bodi pulled away from kissing Michael's ribs. Michael was moaning and wriggling away from Bodi's mouth when Bodi moved to put his lips, without ceremony, around the head of Michael's circumcised cock.

Michael shouted, "Oh God!" and Bodi pulled more of it into his mouth, and still their hands moved, twined together around the shaft, and Bodi sucked down and up on the head until Michael ripped a groan that sounded like it came from his toes. Bodi moved their hands and sucked Michael's cock more than halfway into his mouth.

Peter watched, mesmerized, as Michael screwed his eyes shut and groaned and Bodi bobbed his head some more and tried to swallow. He lost some at the last minute so that when he flopped his head on Michael's stomach, Peter could see the shiny, creamy glaze of it around the few scraggly beard hairs that Bodi was starting to grow.

Bodi was laughing, and Michael tangled his fingers in Bodi's longish blondish hair. "Let me kiss you," he begged, and Bodi looked away and started to wipe his mouth on his shoulder. Michael caught his chin between finger and thumb and said, "No—let me kiss that too!"

They kissed, and it was beautiful. It was deep and passionate, dappled in shadows, and every moment of it made Peter's heart ache.

"It's my turn," Michael murmured, and Bodi shook his head, rolling over to take his weight on his elbow and showing Michael his own erection. Later, Peter would marvel that when Bodi's cock was erect, the foreskin couldn't be seen—it just took up the length of Bodi's shaft and his cock looked a lot like Peter's own. But what fascinated him now was that Bodi's stomach was covered in spunk (that's what the boys called it, right?) and that his cock may still have been erect, but it was growing a little bit softer even as the boys looked.

"Got too excited," Bodi said sheepishly. "Sort of blew my wad when you blew yours."

Michael smiled lazily. "That's actually sort of hot."

Bodi grinned at him, that totally content, serene grin that he gave his sister when she was laughing or that he gave Peter when he'd helped Bodi with math. Except those smiles paled in comparison to what was on Bodi's face when he looked at Peter's cousin, and Peter had to hold back a sob.

Peter wanted to comfort him too. *It's okay, Bodi, I came too, just from watching you. You made me want so badly. It's okay. We're just alike. Nothing's wrong with you.* Except he wanted to do more. Peter wanted to tend to Bodi like Bodi had just tended to Michael. God, Bodi worried so much, took care of so much, wouldn't it be good if someone just… just….

Peter's cock, limp and wet and sticky in his pants, began to stir again as Peter thought of taking Bodi into his mouth, and when he looked through the screen of bushes again to see what they were doing, Michael had Bodi flat on his back and was working his way down Bodi's taut stomach on the way to take care of it.

Peter had seen enough, he thought, his throat sore and his chest aching. Slowly, slowly, he crept away from their spot by the river. He coasted his bike down the hill toward Daisy and got home with an hour to spare before Aunt Aileen got there and demanded to know where the boys had gone.

"I don't know," he told her from his bed. "I've been sick all day."

"You look like you've been crying," she said, frowning.

"I was throwing up," he told her and wondered why right now, on this subject, she actually had to be right.

"I'll go get you some Pepto Bismol," she told him, and it was a relief to drink the nasty stuff because then he *did* feel sick to his stomach, and the lie wasn't such a lie. But after she was gone again and he was alone in his tiny room, he wanted to rage at something, wanted to scream. Because it had been one thing when he thought Michael wasn't doing it right, when he thought Michael hadn't been taking care of Bodi. Peter could want Bodi then, because Peter would do a better job, and Bodi needed someone to take care of him. But Michael took care of him fine—better than fine, it looked like— and that left Peter very much alone.

PETER listened to the shower with that memory so fresh in his mind the edges were bleeding, and found he had to sit down.

Not having Bodi was okay when Michael was taking care of Bodi—but apparently Michael (oh God, Michael—how could you?) hadn't been doing his job. The track marks on Bodi's skin attested to that. But even worse was Bodi's weak and broken smile.

Peter had to fix him. Peter *had* to fix him. And Peter wanted to rage, to howl, to shake his fist at the sky, because Bodi had been beautiful and perfect, unhurt and unscathed, and Michael might have lost his status as the town's golden boy, but he'd had Bodi to protect, and he'd fallen down on the job.

He'd fallen off Peter's pedestal, too, apparently, and Peter had to fight tooth and nail in his chest to see himself ever forgiving his beloved cousin for falling this goddamned far.

CARETAKING

"HEY, Mr. Walters?" Peter's boss at Daisy's only restaurant/diner was usually up at this hour, counting inventory and making sure they had enough to get through the day.

"Yeah?"

"I won't be in tonight. My cousin passed away."

"You're not at home. Why the hell should that matter?"

Peter winced. "I'm telling his friend."

"Families should count more than friends."

"You're not going to give me a goddamned day off to grieve as I see fit?" Peter snarled, and maybe something in his voice was different, because the guy grunted.

"If you don't show up tomorrow, don't show up at all."

"Your goddamned compassion is fucking underwhelming," Peter snarled. "If I don't show up tomorrow, do the town a favor and cook—Daisy's getting crowded." He hit End Call with his heart thundering in his ears, wondering if that meant he'd just quit his job. Some of his adrenaline faded and he put the phone in his pocket, thinking he'd better go in anyway. Proof that good-byes were important was currently getting dressed after a really long shower.

Bodi came out of the bedroom wearing a cleanish pair of coveralls, the top and sides of his hair pulled back in a queue. "So what's up for today?" he asked, and Peter looked into his shadowed eyes.

"Today, I check the want ads for jobs in Arcata," Peter said equably, "especially since my job in Daisy isn't too stable, and then

I'll take a shower and do laundry, and maybe come help you wrench on some bikes."

"Arcata?" Bodi looked surprised, and Peter shrugged.

"I've been deferring my acceptance to Humboldt for ages," he said. "No reason to now. You were right."

Bodi grunted without humor. "You're going to let something *I* said guide a major decision in your life? What in the hell are you thinking?"

Peter shook his head, thinking the lines in Bodi's face had grown even sharper over the years. He'd been, what, twenty-one when he'd been exiled from Daisy? He looked older than twenty-seven now.

"I'm thinking that the one reason I had to hang out in Daisy just stepped on a land mine, that's what I'm thinking."

Bodi's face went waxen, and Peter walked up and grabbed his elbow and then helped him to the stool in front of the kitchen counter.

"I'm sorry," he mumbled.

"You didn't say how," Bodi said back in apology. "I... why does knowing how make it more real?"

Peter didn't say anything. He'd *known* how. He'd lived with it for nearly twenty-four hours now, but nothing had made it as real as the look on Bodi's face.

"I don't know why," Peter whispered after a moment. Bodi seemed to need some sort of answer. Peter moved up tentatively and wrapped his arm around Bodi's shoulders, and Bodi leaned into him without argument.

"You grew taller," Bodi said, half laughing as he looked up. He reached his arm across his chest and clasped Peter's hand. "You grew up taller, but"—and his face darkened and his voice dropped—"you don't look a thing like him."

Peter held him a little tighter. It was true. Michael had been really striking, with short dark hair and big brown eyes. His nose had been bold and his chin had been square, and his eyes had been wide and widely spaced with long black lashes. Peter's hair was straight, more brown than black, and it turned to toffee in the sun. His nose was a knife blade and his chin was a triangle point, and his greenish eyes were more deeply set. Peter had resembled Michael, yes—like cousins do—but no one had ever gotten them mixed up.

"Thank you," Peter said softly, looking down into Bodi's crossed blue eyes.

"You don't want to look like him?" Curiosity, nothing more.

"I don't want you to ever confuse the two of us."

Bodi swallowed and looked away. "You're here, aren't you?"

And Michael was not. Well, it was a start.

"So what are you going to do today again?" Like he'd forgotten. He very probably had—Bodi's mind worked like that, and Peter had never minded repeating himself, even when they'd been young and Bodi had asked him for the third time what he wanted for dinner.

So Peter took a deep breath, revised his original plan, and declared his intention. "Take care of you."

"Very funny." Bodi crossed his arms in front of him on the counter and rested his cheek against his upper arm, looking at Peter sideways. For someone who didn't know him, hadn't seen him do that since adolescence, it might look like he was thinking of going to sleep. Peter knew it was his thinking posture. He wanted to make a list, have things set in his head before he started his day, so he could check the list and the world would make sense.

"Okay, then," Peter said, keeping his arm around Bodi's shoulders. "I'm going to do your laundry, and I'm going to open all your windows and dust. I'm going to change your sheets, and then I'm going to go downstairs and watch you work and see if you need a spare wrench—"

"You still wrench?"

"That piece of shit I own doesn't run on goodwill, Bodi. Yeah. I still wrench. And then, after that, I'm going to make you dinner, and I'm going to sit next to you and watch television until we either scream and cry and get rid of this shit in our chests or just fall asleep."

Bodi turned around and looked at him. "I've done all right for six years," he said, a slight smile touching his mouth. It was real, though, and grateful.

"If I'd known you were alone like this, I would have left at eighteen," Peter said, meaning it.

Bodi shook his head. "I was still waiting for him to come back then," he said, the honesty suddenly heavy and clear like lead crystal in the little room. "I wouldn't have let you."

"Would you have let me two years ago?" Peter asked, almost so angry about this he couldn't breathe.

"I wouldn't have had a choice," Bodi half laughed. "I wasn't doing a lot of decision making myself." He stood then, and Peter was abruptly reminded that he was taller than Bodi, but only by an inch or two. He wasn't sure he'd moved, but suddenly he was just that close, and Bodi smelled clean and looked awake, and his face had color and his eyes were alert and focused very intently on Peter's face, much the way they'd focused on Michael's.

"Time to go, little brother," he said quietly, and Peter's heart throbbed in his ears.

"I'm not your little brother."

Bodi nodded. "I know that, Peter. I've always known it." He leaned forward, and Peter almost closed his eyes, expecting a kiss. But Bodi straightened at the last moment, his lips feathering across Peter's temple. "I'll appreciate the help today, but you don't have to do my laundry. There's some old jeans in my drawers that'll fit you just fine so you don't wreck your clothes."

He turned around and walked out, and Peter looked at him and shook his head. "I'm doing your laundry, dumbass," he said, but he said it quietly and then went to brush his teeth.

PETER spent two hours cleaning the apartment and decided that the place had real potential. No, it wasn't big, but Bodi had put in paneling and the rug was nice—and *God,* the pictures on the walls.

They were all Bodi's, of course, and Peter thought Bodi might sell them at the street fairs that happened up in Mendocino and the other tourist towns down the coast, because he found a whole stack of canvasses—all landscapes—in Bodi's bedroom, along with a computerized list, complete with thumbnail pictures, of paintings that had been sold.

"Go, Bodi!" Peter murmured. All of that color, that brightness, that life—was this what was in Bodi's head underneath the sorrow? Or was this what let him live through the sorrow? Either way, the paintings gave Peter hope.

Bodi's bed was a simple pedestal queen-sized, and Peter went unabashedly snooping through each and every drawer. He told himself it was for stash—especially of the really evil kind that had left those scars on Bodi's arms—but that wasn't what he was looking for.

He was looking for a love life. He found nothing—not a nudie magazine, not a condom, not a packet of lube. He reached too. In the back of an end table he found a crumpled HIV test result dated eighteen months earlier. Negative. Well, that answered *that* question. No sex for Bodi in quite some time. Yeah, well, join the club. Peter would put his twenty-two-year dry spell against Bodi's two years any day.

It wasn't like Peter hadn't had any offers. There were at least fifteen guys in Daisy who had checked him out. The fact that he hadn't ever hidden his gayness like Michael seemed to make them feel like he was giving it out for free.

He wasn't. Michael and Bodi had paid one fucking big badass price for their sexuality. Peter wasn't going to forget that. He was giving it out for love or for nothing at all.

He got into Bodi's old jeans and a grease-stained T-shirt around lunchtime and brought Bodi a couple of sandwiches, which turned out to be lucky, because Bodi had an assistant there with him.

"Thanks, Peter," Bodi said through a full mouth, holding the sandwich in the paper towel it had come in. "This here's Shawn—she's been a real big help."

Shawn was absolutely perfect. She was in her late thirties, built like a fire hydrant, and had the open, smiling face that Joelle had when Joelle *wasn't* looking at Peter.

"Peter," Shawn said, reaching out to shake his hand like a man. "Heard a lot about ya!"

Peter's face went hot. "Yeah, well, I grew out of most of that."

She burst into laughter then and managed to look comically relieved. "Yeah, well, I got a fifteen-year-old boy—I am *so* relieved to hear most of that goes away."

Peter grinned at her, liking her very much, and asked what he could do.

Turned out, a whole lot.

Bodi's business was strictly motorcycles—everything from simple maintenance like changing the oil and checking the timing to the more advanced stuff like chopping the bikes up and changing their shape. You name it, Bodi could do it. He had a couple of special orders he needed to finish by the time he left for Daisy, and he figured he could do it if Peter did the basic stuff.

It was relaxing, Peter thought. Bodi and Shawn played hard rock music loudly, and Peter loved that—he'd always been a fan of Pearl Jam, Nirvana, The Killers, and, oddly enough for the West Coast, Bruce Springsteen. The Boss had always seemed to speak to Bodi's soul in a way that nothing else could, except maybe the landscape around him. Bodi played him every day and knew the lyrics to almost everything he'd put out. Peter had learned to love him because Bodi loved him, and Bodi's music became his.

They called it quits at six, and Shawn looked around and checked their accomplishments off on a list. "Not bad, Bodi. If Peter here can help tomorrow, I think we can have all your orders done before you've got to leave. Why you going back to Daisy again?"

Bodi and Peter looked at each other, and the noisy, productive camaraderie faded. "A funeral," Peter said gruffly, and Bodi wandered to the back of the shop to organize the tools.

Shawn bit her lip and sucked her teeth in worry. She had short-cut dark hair shot with gray. It looked like she tried to dye it on occasion, but she didn't seem the sort of person who was really that vain, the gloves she wore to protect her hands from the grease notwithstanding.

"He's not gonna see that guy who fucked him up two years ago, is he?"

Peter closed his eyes. Details. He wanted details if they shredded his soul. "Only in a pine box," he said bluntly, and her eyes got really big.

"Oh fuck."

"It's in six days. We've got...." He swallowed, thinking of what they were probably going to be doing with Michael's own motorcycle and what it would mean. "We've got our own thing to do."

Shawn nodded and looked uncomfortable. "You—are you... I mean, I've worked for him for three years. That whole time, he's known one person that I think might have been more than a friend. Are you that kind of friend?"

Peter smiled a little, thinking that this right here might be the first place he'd get to say it without censure or people lighting torches and sharpening their pitchforks. "Am I gay too? Yeah."

"But you two...." She trailed off meaningfully, and Peter's face grew warm.

"Have you ever loved someone your whole life?" he asked, and she raised her eyebrows.

"Actually, yeah."

Peter nodded, his eyes tracking Bodi, who had now *truly* become immersed in the task of organizing his tools. "What if he loved someone else?"

"I would have smashed her head in," Shawn said decisively, and Peter found himself laughing humorlessly.

"What if he was your cousin, and you loved him?"

Shawn shook her head. "I got no answer for that."

"Yeah. I didn't like mine much either."

Peter went up the stairs then to shower and make dinner, and Bodi was done with work and taking a shower as Peter was plating the pasta. They ate on the coffee table, and then Bodi said, "Grab your jacket."

Peter didn't even ask why.

They trotted down the stairs in the twilight of early spring, and Peter caught his breath with the beauty of the scarlet sun trapped between the gray sky and silvering water. Bodi turned directly up the road toward the ocean and kept walking, quickly enough that Peter would have been winded if he didn't run on his own. The waves were coming up, high tide, a heaving mass of heft and surf, the constant hum that drove the world this close to the ocean. The highway ran close to the shore for a good mile or two, and Bodi followed it tonight while the sun and sea turned to blood and exploded out on the horizon.

They walked in silence, and Peter let Bodi just look out on the sand, those eyes wide and simply drinking the world in. Peter stared out with him and started imagining the surf, foaming about his chest and then receding, pulling out six—hell, twelve—years of pain and yearning with it.

"After I got back from rehab," Bodi said, his voice low and rumbly, like the surf itself, "I was about jumping out of my fucking skin. Those first three days, the damned garage wasn't even open— Shawn had taken it over, and she was on vacation, and I didn't know anything that was going on. So I had nothin' to do. I couldn't read—

it ain't never been easy for me, and my brain was just so jumpy. I just couldn't make myself do it right then. I... I couldn't paint, right? 'Cause anything I tried... it just came out red and black and shit colored, and I hated that, hated that crap was inside me, so I just didn't do it. And... I think my first thought was just to run out and find a dealer, you know? I'd wrecked the bike, it was in the garage, and I knew enough that as shaky as I was just from *wanting* it, I shouldn't be riding, so I think I was just going to go running for a bar and find the first person with... fuck. I was doing heroin, but I would have taken anything by then, right?"

Peter swallowed, keeping his feet moving in time with Bodi's. They'd probably walked about three miles by now, and Bodi stopped abruptly and turned toward the last sliver of crimson sun. "Yeah."

Bodi looked at him and then nodded out to the ferocious roar of the surf as it tried to gobble more and more sand with every heave and swell. "I found myself out here."

"It's beautiful." There was no lie in that.

Bodi nodded. "Yeah. And by the time the sun was down and the waves had reached the breakwater and were coming back down...." He sighed, and he leaned a little, his hand brushing Peter's. Peter took it as a sign and wrapped his fingers around Bodi's work-roughened, stringy fingers, and then Bodi adjusted his grip and twined their hands together tighter.

"It saved you," Peter said softly.

"You give thanks to the things that save you," Bodi acknowledged, and then he turned, and they walked back to Bodi's garage in the dark without another word.

They watched television on the couch like Peter had planned, and Bodi rested in his arms without protest. When the last show was over and it was only the news, Peter turned off the TV (because they hadn't liked it as kids and he didn't think that had changed any), and they listened to the oceanic hush for a moment.

"Why did he leave?" Peter murmured, thinking it was time to ask.

Not for Bodi. "He...." Bodi shrugged. "Can we talk about it some other time?" he asked plaintively, and he sounded mostly asleep. "I ain't felt this peaceful in forever."

Peter hmmed in his throat. They'd kicked off their shoes, and the pillow and the blankets were at his end of the couch. He leaned back, putting his head on the pillow and pulling Bodi down until his head tucked just right there on Peter's shoulder. If Peter pushed back and they both stayed sideways, Bodi wouldn't fall off the couch.

"Bodi?" Peter asked, wondering if he was still awake, and Bodi hmmed back. "Bodi, did you have any idea how much I loved you when we were growing up?"

"No," Bodi said, mostly asleep now. "Too bad you can't love me anymore."

Peter was stunned, and Bodi's soft snores breathed against his sleeve. "I do!" Peter whispered, knowing Bodi couldn't hear. "God, Bodi, do you think I could ever stop?"

But Bodi didn't answer, and Peter was ready to close his eyes too.

IN THE afternoon, Peter drove straight from Bodi's house to his job at the Daisy Diner and arrived there about three minutes before he was supposed to clock in. He ran through the back, grabbing a clean apron and his time card and then rounding the corner and punching the card in the electronic clock.

"You're—"

"Exactly on time," Peter said, looking at Mr. Walters with unfriendly eyes. The guy—Joelle's husband, actually—had hired him on the understanding that it was doing God's work to hire the rejected and the outcast. Besides, what Peter paid Aileen in rent went to help the church. It was only charitable.

The only reason Peter hadn't been consigned to the serfdom of busboy for the past six years was that he'd gone in to cook one day when the regular daytime cook, Eschenger, had been home because he was having some sort of gastric attack, and it turned out Peter was pretty damned good at his job. Mr. Walters called it "some sort of gay thing," which made Peter crack up, because he read all the e-books he could afford, and *those* gay men all seemed to live on takeout. Anyway, Peter was pretty good at it—in fact, he knew a couple of the town's residents came in to eat regularly, but only when he was there to cook. He got tips from those folks, which was nice because it made saving up for school a lot easier, but judging from the look on Walters's face, being his only competent cook wasn't enough anymore.

"I say you're late. Lateness gets you fired." Walters was a white, balding, fortyish, paunchy man with bitter lines at his mouth and eyes. If he wore anything but chef whites, greasy and underwashed, Peter had never seen it.

Peter rolled his eyes and held up the receipt he'd pulled out and hadn't yet discarded. "This says I'm on time, which means I've got a case in any court in the country." Not that he would have taken it that far, but the fact that he was right, and Walters couldn't seem to see it was chafing up his body from his balls to his stomach to the back of his spine.

Walters curled his lip up and snarled. "You got your aunt here, grieving, and you spend two days at that no-good faggot's place—"

Peter hit him, and *that's* how he quit his job.

He hadn't been in a fight since middle school, but his arm cocked back and his fist connected with Walters's paunchy jaw, and Walters went crashing back against the wall by the dish stand—and came up swinging. He broke Peter's nose with a hammy fist in an explosion of blinding pain that might have rocked him on any other day, but not now, not when the last two days had been spent swimming in a never-ending masochistic emotional swamp. Today, it just pissed him off. He swung two more times, connecting with the man's nose and cutting his knuckles on Walters's teeth. Walters went down, grunting, and slid back against the wall to the floor, and Peter was still pissed. He grabbed a clean sauté pan from the rack and hurled it with all his force against the wall above the dish stand, where it clanged, denting the wall, changing the face of it forever. Peter howled, blood pouring down his face, and then glared at the ten or so people peering in over the counter to the back of the kitchen.

"This town doesn't have *anything* to say to Bodi Kovacs," he shouted. "Anyone who thinks they got somethin' to say, they need to go through me, and I'm still pissed!"

He aimed a kick at Walters's thigh then, and turned it at the last moment to connect weakly with the wall. Walters glared up at him but didn't try to get up.

"Have fun finding a replacement, asshole," Peter snapped. "If you don't have my last check ready by the day before the funeral, I'll fucking sue you."

Empty threat, of course. Peter grabbed his jacket from the hook where he'd just left it and turned around and stalked out of the employee entrance. He wondered if Walters would call the cops. It was a possibility, but he doubted it. For one thing, there were ten witnesses who would say Walters had been an asshole at the beginning, and that he'd fought back. For another, if Walters went to the cops, he'd have to admit in writing that he got his ass beat by a faggot, and Peter didn't think that was happening either.

So he pulled his car into the carport of his Aunt Aileen's house wearing Bodi's old jeans, old briefs, a T-shirt, his own jacket, and a giant bloody mask from his throbbing nose. He hoped he scared the hell out of her.

He clattered into the kitchen, turned on the light, and walked straight for the ice and the ibuprofen. He could see the television flicker from the darkness of the living room and was not surprised when Aileen walked into the kitchen in full cry.

"Where in the hell have you been?" she asked. "Leaving me all alone—what happened to you?"

Peter let out a grunt of laughter. "Quit my job."

"Why in the hell did you do that? Who else is going to hire you in this town?"

"Since I'm moving on Sunday, I guess it doesn't matter," Peter said. His voice was muffled from the swelling in his nose, and he felt a sudden shaft of vanity. Dammit, he wanted Bodi to *see* him. Yeah, Peter was moving to Arcata—this *wasn't* his last chance, but…

But after falling asleep on the couch last night, Bodi had woken him up sometime later and said, "C'mon. The bed's big enough for two."

They'd slept in their T-shirts and underwear, but Peter had wrapped his arms around Bodi's chest just like he had when they'd been on the narrow couch, and Bodi had let him. Peter woke up with a warm armful of man, a hard, stringy, resilient man who looked like an angel when his eyes were closed and even more like one when they were open, and Peter hadn't wanted to wake up anywhere else in the world. He'd taken advantage then, kissed Bodi's forehead as he slept, and then tangled their legs together and felt Bodi against him, full length, and shivered just from the decadence of having that much flesh in contact.

Bodi woke up and looked at him with those shadowed, guileless blue eyes. "It's been a while," he said, smiling apologetically and shifting so his morning wood wasn't grinding up against Peter's.

"Try never," Peter said, pulling Bodi close again.

Bodi's eyes widened. "Twenty-two, Petey, and never been kissed?"

"I'm picky," Peter said soberly, and Bodi grimaced.

"Just blind."

Peter shook his head and reached up to push the fall of gold-brown hair out of Bodi's face. "I see exactly who you are."

Bodi closed his eyes and pushed his face toward Peter's, first pressing their mouths together and then pulling Peter's lower lip between his own and sucking softly. He let go and smiled a little. "I'm the guy who gave you your first kiss," Bodi said, and his smile was as winsome as a child's.

Peter was still stunned as Bodi rolled out of bed and stretched, then made his way to the shower. Peter wanted to go brush his teeth and do it again, but for the rest of the day, Bodi pretended it hadn't happened at all.

He pretended right up until Peter stopped working and got ready to go. Bodi walked out to the car as Peter clattered down the stairs.

"I'll be at Aunt Aileen's," Peter said, looking at Bodi, who was rubbing at his hands disconsolately with a garage towel.

Bodi opened his mouth to say something and then closed it. "I'll meet up with you there," he said. He sighed. "I'll just act like I'm camping, okay? We'll just assume I'll be staying out by the swimming hole—are kids still going out there these days?"

Peter shook his head. "Too cold right now. In another month, you'da had company, but not right now."

Bodi nodded. "Copacetic. I've got a sleeping bag, small ice chest."

"I'll bring you food," Peter said and then blew out a breath. "This is stupid. Won't your mom—"

Bodi shook his head and looked away. "I send her Christmas cards," he said, embarrassed. "She sends 'em back."

Peter nodded, his chest suddenly so clogged with hatred that he couldn't bear to look at Bodi, like he was going to profane the man with all of that bitterness. "I'll be coming out here, looking for a place," he said. "Time for me to start school."

The naked hope on Bodi's face was like an acid bath. It hurt—oh God, it hurt—but it cleansed that acrid patina of hatred away too. "I'll... I can help," he said, and Peter smiled. *Help by letting me live here, in this snug little apartment, where your handprint is everywhere. God, Bodi, I don't even know what I want to do in school, but I* need *to take care of you.*

They did that man thing again—clasped hands, moved their shoulders in—and Peter couldn't stand just doing that, so he took his other hand and captured the back of Bodi's head, and pushed his mouth against Bodi's and forced it open for a kiss.

Bodi grunted and relaxed, and their hands were still clasped between them, but Bodi's shoulders melted into Peter's body, like he belonged in Peter's arms. He returned the kiss, taking Peter's tongue, giving his own, finally, pushing Peter back against the car and unclasping their hands, splaying his hand over Peter's throat and holding Peter in place and kissing him until every muscle in Peter's body went taut and then relaxed.

Bodi pulled back then and tried to control his breathing. "Peter... Peter, I take this shit seriously."

"You think I don't?"

Bodi closed his eyes. "Yeah. Maybe we shouldn't—"

Peter wasn't going to hear how that sentence ended. "I'll see you tomorrow," he said. Then he kissed Bodi on the mouth just hard and long enough for Bodi to know that he meant it. He got in the car and cranked the stereo all the way back to Daisy, and he thought he had all his anger, all his venom, out of his system then.

Until he beat the hell out of his boss, that is.

And now, looking at Aunt Aileen, he found that it was still there. Well, a six-year backlog—might take some mighty hearty soul scrubbing to get rid of that shit.

"You're leaving me?" Aileen said, her voice the epitome of hurt, and Peter didn't want to talk to her anymore for the rest of his life.

"You don't give a shit if I'm here," he said, applying the ice to his nose. "Hell, Aileen, now that Michael's not sending you *my goddamned money* anymore, you don't have a reason for me to stay."

Aileen's eyes got big. "How did you—"

"How do you think?" Peter turned his head and spit blood down the sink because he was tired of swallowing it. "Really, do you think you drive a kid out of town with guilt for something he didn't do, and he just fucking goes away? He didn't for Michael. Michael might have steered clear of this suck-ass town when he was on leave, but he came back for Bodi." Peter wasn't going to tell her that Michael's attention had been worse for Bodi than his indifference might have been. He wanted her to hurt. Dammit, she *deserved* to hurt. "He told Bodi everything."

Aileen's big-eyed look had turned to defiance. "So what if I did keep it? What if I did give it to the church? He just kept sending it to me, telling me to make sure you were taken care of. I took care of your soul, that's what I did! That was the devil's money—that boy didn't know what he was doing, giving it to you, signing up for the military. He was just trying to steer clear of the evil inside him—"

"They were *kids!*" Peter cried, closing his eyes against tears and telling himself it was the pain in his head. "Jesus, Aileen—if they'd been…." His throat closed against the names, because that hatred was just not going anywhere. "If they'd been any other couple in this mud puddle, Michael would have been knocked up by his senior year and we would have had a wedding!"

Aileen's hand connected with his cheek then, sending shockwaves through his face. For a moment—a bare moment—he almost forgot she wasn't a paunchy human tractor like Walters, and almost hit her in return. Her hand pulled back for one more slap, and Peter caught her wrist.

"I'll be out of this place the day of the funeral," he said. "And Bodi's going to be coming in and out. Shut the hell up and leave him alone. We're having our own sendoff for Michael, and you don't got a say."

"I should kick you out right the hell—"

"Do it, and I'll tell the whole world that you stole my college money, Aileen. You had written proof of what Michael wanted that money for. I'll go tell the church that you're a thief. I mean, I know they don't give a fuck, because apparently even though the ten commandments don't say a goddamned thing about it, we all know a faggot's worse than a thief, but do you want the whole town to know it? Do you want them all to know you stole from me when I was underage? Do they all know I'm payin' rent? You go ahead and ride all this 'poor, poor Aileen' bullshit you've got coming in. You go bathe in your son's blood like it makes you a better person. We both know the truth. We know what you did, we know what you said to Michael that day, and we know why he would rather go out and die for his country than come back and live here—or even come back and take care of Bodi, goddammit, because that's what he should have been doing. So you go play that card, Aileen, I'm not gonna stop you. But I'm going to say good-bye to your son, and I'm going to take care of his lover, and you just shut the fuck up about it!"

Aileen had turned white while he was snarling, and she'd pulled her hand out of his grasp to put it up in front of her mouth. She'd tried to say his name a couple of times, like there was tenderness between them, but he didn't feel it, and he was tired and heartsore and pissed off, so he wasn't going to fake it.

He turned again and hawked some more blood, thankful that the bleeding was slowing down, and then turned on the tap to wash it down the drain.

"I'm gonna go take a shower before I go out to the garage," he said. "Try not to steal the change out of my wallet while it's hanging in the room I pay you for."

"I won't touch any of your stuff, you worthless faggot!" she snapped, but she was sobbing, so even the bitter epithet lost some of its power. "How can you be so mean, Peter James Armbruster? I'm in *mourning*!"

"Yeah?" Peter snapped from the doorway. "Who are you grieving for? Because it sure as hell isn't your son! You woulda had to know him to be sad about him, and you didn't want to know him at all. But you know something? The rest of us might have. I think he would have been a damned fine person to know. But I think you washed away the good parts of him, too, so we don't even have that."

He left her there, crying helplessly, not wanting to explain another damned thing to her, and went upstairs to change.

BURNING BRIDGES

IN AUGUST, two months before Bodi's sister hung herself using a triple length of clothesline from the garage, Michael dumped his bike taking a turn too fast. He almost killed himself—it had been a toss-up whether he'd slide headfirst into a granite wall or off the edge of the road altogether. He chose off the edge of the road altogether and broke his arm, dislocated his shoulder, and scraped the hell out of his whole upper body. Bodi had needed to pick him up out of the underbrush and put him on the back of Bodi's bike to take him to the hospital, and by the time Peter and his aunt had gotten there, Bodi had been a wreck.

Peter remembered sitting next to him while he'd scrubbed his face with shaking hands, muttering a macabre list to himself. "Stop the bike, go back, look over the edge, is he okay? Pick him up, pull his bike off the road, oh God, his helmet's cracked, oh thank God for the fucking helmet, go straight, thirty miles, keep going, Michael, wake up, can't sleep...." And so on, until Peter pushed Bodi's head onto his own shoulder and wrapped an arm around his body. Bodi had just huddled there, crying softly. It had been awkward and embarrassing. Bodi had been twenty and Peter not quite sixteen, and Bodi had always been the grown-up, but not on this day.

The adults had been okay with it, actually. Aileen and Bodi's mom, Cynthia, seemed to feel that it was all part of growing up, this wrecking your bike on Highway 122. Peter wanted to scream at them, because it felt like they weren't seeing Bodi disintegrate before their eyes, but before he could, Bodi stood up and went and asked how Michael was doing, and offered everyone coffee, and it was all fine.

Well, sort of. The guys didn't get to sneak out of church for two more months, and Michael's bike? Well, it was going to need some solid work before it was rideable again. After Michael used his mother's car to sneak out of town to set Bodi up in Arcata and sign up for the military, he fixed up Peter's car so Peter could get his license. *That's* what he drove before his final goodbye, because otherwise, that fucked-up motorcycle was all he had. A month later, when he left for good? They had no idea he was leaving. They hadn't had any idea where he'd gone the first time. It wasn't until he'd exited the country and left that pithy, damning letter telling them which unit he'd be in and when he'd be deployed, that they even knew he'd gone to see the recruiter at all.

So Peter sojourned to the disused garage to confront the motorcycle, so to speak. It needed to be fixed before they did what needed to be done—and not just fixed. Fixed up in style. The fact that they were going to ride it just to kill it wasn't a consideration. It was the last thing left of the smiling, animated, gentle boy they'd both known. It had to look like that boy. It had to be bright and shining and whole.

It hadn't been touched since the tow truck had brought it back while Michael was still in the hospital, getting his arm plastered. Michael and Bodi had been planning to fix it up themselves, but, well, that thing happened that no one wanted to talk about, and there it sat, a festering wreck, quietly screaming into the dust that things were meant to be better.

It had sat there for over six years.

That night, after the argument with Aileen, Peter managed to dismantle half of it before he went to bed, still-bleeding nose and all. He put the pieces into two piles—broken and whole. There was a whole lot there that was broken, but there was a surprising amount that was salvageable and could be put back right. Peter hoped it was a sign.

The next day, he was in the middle of cleaning and reassembling the carburetor when there was a metal roar of a motorcycle outside the garage. Peter kept on working, and he wasn't

61

really surprised when Bodi walked in, but he didn't turn around, either.

"You started?"

"Yup."

"What about work?"

Peter turned and looked at him with raised eyebrows over his swollen nose and the two black eyes that went with it.

"Oh, *dude!*" Bodi walked closer and took off his riding gloves, suddenly right in front of Peter and putting gentle fingers on the sides of his nose, which had been throbbing all night. "Dude, you need to have this set. You up for it?"

Peter grimaced. "No. Fuckin' hurts!"

Bodi cupped his cheek then, a gesture of tenderness, and Peter pressed his hand against it to keep it there. Bodi came a little closer and sighed. He smelled like exhaust from the bike, and like ocean and forest wind, and his blue eyes were sad as he pursed his lips in sympathy.

"Go get some ice, Petey. Don't fight me on this, 'kay?"

Peter would have scowled, but he knew from his past twelve hours' experience just trying on the expression would make his eyes water. "Yeah," he sighed, and he walked in through the kitchen to throw some ice in a towel and take another round of ibuprofen before Bodi set his nose.

Joelle Walters was sitting at the kitchen table, and she scowled at him as he worked.

"No less than you deserve," she humphed, and Peter rolled his eyes. He was going to say something really heroic, like "Fuck you, bitch!" and then he saw Lucy sitting in the living room again, waving shyly at him. He ignored Joelle and waved a little bit at Lucy, and then went back to his ice.

"You're not even going to answer me?" she snapped as he hit the door, and he turned back around.

"What is it you expect from us, Joelle? You're all coming in here, consoling Aileen and pretending it's not your fault. You *broke* them. Something really awful happened, and instead of banding together and comforting people, you staged a witch hunt and *broke* them. All of you. The whole damned town. And I watched. You all made it *really clear* that the only reason I had a place to live was because of Aunt Aileen's *charity*—I felt like I had no choice. I've got a choice now. And I choose to tell you all to take this shitty town and eat it. And if you think that makes me a weak faggot, go look at your husband's face—it can't possibly look better than mine."

"The good Lord says to turn the other cheek—"

"Yeah, but you're the people who say it's wrong to take it up the ass." Oh God. Lucy was looking at him with big eyes, and he didn't want to do this in front of her. She had a good life here, and she believed she was loved. Peter couldn't take that from her—he couldn't. It hurt something in him, to think he'd strip a child of that one thing he'd never had. Peter grabbed his ice, whirled around, and walked out. He took great satisfaction in slamming the door with unnecessary force.

Bodi was walking around the bike, talking quietly to himself as Peter walked in. "Disconnect the exhaust manifold, replace the exhaust pipe, patch the gas tank, pound out the forks, need a new front tire...." He looked up as Peter walked in, and squinted. "Your face is all blotchy. Who'd you yell at?"

Peter's face probably got blotchier. "Joelle was in there." He grimaced. "I'm sort of in the process of burning all my bridges."

Bodi blinked. "Why would you want to do that?"

"Because I should have done it six years ago. Are you going to set my nose or what?" He needed to hawk blood in the worst way.

Bodi's hands on his face were tender, gentle around his cheeks as he framed Peter's nose with his thumbs and jerked quickly. Peter grunted and closed his eyes against a simply *gorgeous* painflower, and squinted at Bodi through his blurred vision.

63

Bodi stroked his cheek for a moment and tousled his hair. "You were always such a tough kid," he said with a small smile. "Tough but quiet. Just sat there, all big eyes—Michael used to call it your potato face. Can't believe you grew up to be such a rabble-rouser."

Peter looked away. "I should have defended you," he said, his voice small.

Bodi's hand never moved from his cheek. "We never blamed you," he said seriously, but Peter shook his head.

"You should have, Bodi. You should have blamed somebody. You should have done anything but disappear to Arcata and let Michael—"

Bodi shook his head, smacking Peter's cheek gently. "Don't finish that," he said and, just that quickly, turned back to the motorcycle.

"Oil, spark plugs, arc welder, gloves, mask...." The list went on, and Peter trotted back into the house and into his room to get a piece of paper and a pen. He thought he'd made it out without anybody seeing him until he turned around, and there was Lucy, trotting at his heels.

"You're mad at my mom," she said as he neared the garage, and he grunted.

"I'm sorry you heard that."

"Why are you mad?"

Peter sighed. "She was mean to a friend of mine." He walked into the garage where Bodi had the bike and the parts on a tarp and was continuing on where Peter left off.

"Is that him?"

"Yeah," Peter said, and then he sat on the little stool and started writing things down. "Bodi, this is Lucy—Lucy, this is Bodi."

Lucy blinked. "I like your name," she said. "Why is my mom mean to you?"

Bodi looked at her, at a loss. "Peter...," he said helplessly, and Peter looked at her, too, and shrugged.

"Bodi and I are gay," he said, and Bodi grunted.

"God, really? You're gonna just tell a kid that!"

Peter chuffed out a puff of air. "It's not dirty, Bodi. It just frickin' is."

"Yeah," he said, wrenching hard on the gas tank to get it off the frame. "I just wish it was just frickin' my own damned business."

"What's gay?" Lucy asked, and Peter wrote down a few more items for their buy list before he answered.

"It means we like to kiss other boys instead of girls," Peter said, and he was not prepared to hear her giggle.

"You mean like Kurt from *Glee*?"

"Yeah," Bodi said, surprising Peter even more. "'Cept I'm too dumb to go to that fancy school, and Peter can't sing for shit."

Lucy looked at him curiously, and Peter said, "Don't listen to him, Lucy. He's real smart. He reads poetry and stuff."

"Slowly," Bodi muttered, and Peter ignored him.

"But he is right about my singing," Peter continued. "I'm bad." And then he launched into the theme from SpongeBob SquarePants to make her giggle.

She was a great kid, quiet, attentive. They sat her up on Peter's stool and let her doodle on the rest of Peter's notebook while they continued to take apart the bike and make a list of things they'd need. Some of the stuff they'd be able to get at the auto shop in town, but most of it, Bodi would have to drive back to Arcata to get.

"You can take my car," Peter said, and Bodi nodded.

"How about you go into town first to see what they've got," he said. "I'll stay here and fix up the rest."

"Can I do something?" Lucy asked, and Peter had an idea. He got some clean rags and a little bit of vinegar, then set her by the fender and the one good fork. "Clean these," he said. "Polish them up fancy. They're going to a funeral."

She did, singing to herself as she went, something about a pony and pink and rainbows, and Peter half laughed to himself as he turned to make the trip to town. Then he saw the look on Bodi's face and stopped laughing.

Bodi was on his knees, wrenching on something that needed his leverage, but he'd stopped. He was looking at the little girl with a look of such profound grief that Peter's heart stopped with his laughter.

"Bodi," he murmured, "do you want me to ask her to leave?"

Bodi shook his head. "Leave her," he said, his voice rough. "Shawn's got a daughter, but it still feels like I haven't heard that sound in a long time." He didn't object when Peter squatted down next to him and kissed his temple softly.

"I'm sorry," Peter said, his voice low, and Bodi leaned into him.

"Thank you. Now go get that list, okay?"

"Yeah."

Peter walked out and hopped in the car, not wanting to tell Bodi the bad news about this little trip. Bodi wouldn't know that Warren Drescher worked at Daisy's one auto parts store, and Peter wouldn't tell him.

Fortunately Nate Lombard was there too. Peter had damned near forgotten that, and as he walked in, he had the dizziest memory.

JUNIOR high was a little slice of hell.

When Peter was in the sixth grade, not long after he, Michael, and Bodi had gone swimming together, a seventh grader had walked by him, tripped him, and called him "faggot."

66

Peter remembered that moment. It came a few weeks after he'd started dreaming about Bodi, and he remembered a promise he'd made his mother. He pulled himself out of mud. Then he picked up the remnants of his lunch and threw them in the trashcan with as much dignity as he could muster.

"What?" the older kid snapped. "You got nothin' to say?"

Peter turned around and looked the kid in the face. "I may be a faggot," he said clearly, "but at least I'm not a moron, an asshole, or a rednecked motherfucker."

That was the first time Michael had to help him up out of the trashcan.

A grand total of twenty-six people graduated from the K-8 school in Peter's year, walking across the high school football field dressed in new church dresses and new church suits. They said a prayer before and after, like it was still 1950 or something. By the time they did that, all but one of those kids had, at one time or another, thrown wadded-up paper at Peter or tripped him or spilled something on him or called him a faggot under their breath. The teachers told him that all he had to do was deny it, and Peter told them that all they had to do was say it wasn't okay. Nobody liked that answer, but it didn't matter. The students got to pick their order in which to walk across the little portable stage as their name was called, and Peter took his place at the end of the line—the better to not be picked on when no one could see.

Right in front of him was a kid with sandy-blond hair and unremarkable green eyes. Peter knew his name—how could he not? But as they all stood nervously and watched much of the town file in to sit in the bleachers, Nate turned to him with a nervous smile.

"I hate all these people looking at me," he said softly, and Peter nodded.

"At least they're not throwing shit," he said, glaring at one of his worst tormenters—a snotty dark-haired girl who sang in the church choir and who stuck her tongue out at him even as he watched—and Nate nodded.

"Yeah, well, she's gonna end up knocked up at sixteen. We'll have the option of laughing our asses off."

It was one of those moments when you realize that your world may suck, but other people's do too. "She threw shit at you?"

Nate wrinkled his nose. "Oreos. Jesus, just because that skinny bitch don't want to eat them don't mean I want that shit in my hair!"

Peter nodded. "Well, I'm lucky," he admitted.

Nate looked into the audience, where Michael, Bodi, and Bodi's sister all sat near the front. Michael gave Peter a little wave, and Peter waved back.

"You got guardian angels," Nate said with some envy, and Peter had to agree.

"Yeah," he said and realized how grateful he really was for Bodi's not-so-subtle intervention in sixth grade. "So, next year. Maybe we sit together and everyone else leaves you alone."

Nate looked at him with shining eyes. "God, it would be nice to not have my iPod stolen," he said fervently, and Peter suddenly thought he might survive high school. The loudspeaker buzzed then, and they didn't get a chance to say anything, but the next year, Peter looked around at lunch.

Nate had saved a place for him in a tiny table almost invisible in the far corner of the quad. Peter made his way there and glared at anyone who got in his way.

NATE looked up when Peter walked in, and his eyes widened in apparent surprise. Peter gave him a lame smile, because Nate might not have any more fond memories of Peter left, but he was surprised.

"Hey," Nate said softly. "I was really sorry to hear about Michael."

Peter swallowed. Oh hell. He hadn't been expecting humanity. He should have. Nate hadn't been the one who'd left Peter in the cold in the first place, but still.

Peter swallowed and tried for grace. "Thank you," he murmured. "That's nice of you to say. We're actually fixing up his bike."

"Wow, Pete. That's a big job—you showed it to me, remember? Let me see what you need."

It was so matter-of-fact, and that made it easier. Peter walked up to the counter and gave him the list.

Nate scanned it, and he grimaced. "Geez—we're not going to have a lot of this shit!"

"Yeah, I know—but if you could mark what you've got and get it for me, we can go into town and get the rest tomorrow."

Nate sucked his teeth and ran a hand through his already thinning sandy-brown hair. "We could order it in, is that okay?"

Peter shook his head. "Sort of a time crunch. This is just to get us started—"

"Who's this we?" Warren asked, walking up from the back of the shop, where he'd apparently been hiding under a rock. "You keep sayin' 'we' like there's somethin' we don't know, Armbruster. The whole town knows he's here."

Warren was a big guy—six five to Peter's five ten or so—and Peter would be hard put to best him in a fight. "Good for you, Warren. You can recognize a motorcycle. Given what you do for a living, I'd say that'd be a plus."

"He's not wanted here!"

Nate bobbed his head nervously. "I'm just going to go get what we've got for you, Peter, okay?"

"Yeah, Nate, thanks." *Way to commit, there, buddy.* But again, he'd had a chance to gain Nate's loyalty, and he'd blown it off. He'd gotten a smile and some help—maybe *that* was where he should focus that gratitude the church was always talking about.

"I mean, what's he doing back here?" Warren asked, not moving as Nate went to brush by him on the way to the stock room. Nate finally just put a hand on that massive shoulder and shoved, and Warren bared his teeth in response.

"My dad owns the shop, Warren," Nate said finally. "He may like you, but if we get into a fight, there goes your job. Leave him alone."

Warren stepped aside and let Nate pass, but he was by no means done with Peter yet.

"Answer me!" Warren snapped, and Peter realized how free he'd felt since the night before. He'd lived in this town for twelve years. He'd been called "faggot" behind his back and to his face. He'd been told the whole time that he should be grateful—oh so grateful—for three squares and a roof over his head and someone to teach him right from wrong. As it turned out, the best thing this town had ever given him was the thing it had destroyed without a backward glance. *Oh Michael—you shouldn't have had to die to set me free.*

"He's come to mourn his friend," Peter said. "You got anything against that?"

"Don't you mean his *girl*friend?" Warren sneered, and Peter's whole body went cold.

"No, Warren, his *boy*friend. Didn't anyone explain how that works? Oh wait, no. You had to go see for yourself and then tell the whole town. Now why was that again?" Peter pretended to think when this, this most basic injustice, had actually been waiting to spew forth with steam and bile for six years.

"Shut up, faggot," Warren snapped, and Peter suddenly didn't care how big Warren was, didn't care that his face was still throbbing from the night before, and didn't even care about the distinctive clatter of Bodi's motorcycle outside the parts store as he talked: he wanted pain, and he wanted blood, and he wanted it *now*!

"'Shut up, faggot'? Is that all you've got?" Peter was leaning up against the counter, his voice shaking too hard for him to scream.

70

"You and your girlfriend let a girl *die* on your watch, and all you got in response is 'Shut up, faggot'? That's it? Not an 'I'm sorry'? Not a 'You know, we were getting paid to watch somebody and we fucked up'? I mean, no one blames you for fucking up—it wasn't an easy gig, but seriously—"

Warren lunged over the counter and grabbed his T-shirt, then hauled him up close for a little face to face, and Peter? He went. He got right there and forced this man—God, it was so easy to think of him as a monster, but he was really just a man—to say it. To make whatever justification he could, because Peter was *done* giving people excuses for the bullshit they'd been telling themselves.

"We weren't the queers fucking in the woods, asshole!" Warren snarled, and Peter's vision went red, just like it had with Walters, except he actually used his words this time.

"No, you were the guy playing grabass with his girlfriend when she had a fucking responsibility. Are you ever going to admit that? *You and Ashley fucked up!* Bodi was *paying* you to watch his sister—*paying* you. How can you blame Bodi for what happened? Why does this whole town think that being gay is a worse sin than fucking up?"

He was shouting and—oh fuck—he was crying. Warren had backed up, let go of his shirt, was looking at him with shell-shocked eyes, like this was something he hadn't wanted to admit and here Peter was, being cruel enough to spell it out.

"We didn't fuck up," he whispered, and Peter felt a hand on his arm, pulling at him, and he almost shook it off.

"You did too. It was your fault. And no one would have held it against you," Peter said, some of the anger leaching away. "No one. No one should have held it against anyone."

He turned to Bodi, who had magically appeared in the parts store just when Peter needed him most, and was now pulling urgently at his arm.

Nate came around with the list and said, "I'll bring this to your house, Peter," really quiet like, and Peter said, "I haven't paid."

Nate just shook his head and glared at Warren. "I'll bring it by your house. No worries"—and Bodi pulled Peter out of the store before he could get into the second fight in two days.

"I'm sorry," Peter said needlessly as the doorbell jangled behind them.

Bodi shook his head, wrapping an arm around Peter's shoulders. "You're not the one who should be sorry."

"But I am." Peter passed his hand under his eyes. "I am."

"Your aunt's friend got sort of pissed," Bodi told him, like salt was needed in the wound. "I guess she thought I wasn't safe to leave her kid with."

Peter flattened his palms against his eyes and screamed, right there in the parking lot. Bodi's arm tightened around his shoulders, and Peter screamed and screamed again, the sounds ripping his throat, rending the still air of the little town. The parts store was on the east end of Zinnia, the main street, and Peter removed his hands and looked on blearily as the good people of Daisy stuck their heads out of their little storefronts or pressed their faces against their windows or looked through the blinds. *Come see us! Come see the only two fags on the planet of Daisy!*

"Don't get mad," Bodi said tensely, looking around them, seeing the same faces Peter was. "Don't get mad. Don't get mad, dammit, or I'll get mad too. I can't get mad, Peter, okay? I can't. C'mon."

It was the shaking in his voice that got to Peter. Bodi had been broken, and he knew his limits. Peter accepted that guiding arm on his shoulder steering him to where Bodi's cruising Harley— complete with old-style leather saddlebags on frames and airbrushing on the fenders and shiny chrome glass-pack mufflers— sat warming in the spring sun.

For a moment, Peter was distracted by the magpie shininess of chrome and the solidity of well-loved machine, and his anger was absorbed by Bodi's warm, forgiving arm.

"Where we going?" he asked.

"Swimming hole," Bodi said, his face closed. "As good a place as any to cool down."

There was an extra helmet hooked to the bitch-seat bar, brown with blue stripes, and Peter recognized it as the one he'd used when he was a kid. He'd sold his bike, a barely street legal little universal Japanese make, about two years after Michael had left town because he'd never ridden it, but the helmet—that, he'd kept. As he put it on, it felt like the helmet was the last straw, the final barrier between Peter and the memory the whole town had been trying to forget.

PETER didn't miss nearly as much church as Bodi and Michael, but he missed some.

The first time he caught them deliberately, he'd been planning to play it cool—just breeze in being loud and surprise them, so they knew their place wasn't as invisible as they thought it was. But he'd found himself walking quietly anyway. He neared his spot in stealth mode, and by the time he got to the screen of leaves, he was walking low to the ground and listening for their noises.

He got there late this time—they were both sprawled out over the sleeping bag, Michael on his stomach with his knees splayed widely, Bodi lying sideways, covering Michael's shoulders with his own, stroking a hand down Michael's lower back. There was a cream-colored trickle coming from Michael's backside and coating his thighs, and for a moment, Peter was mesmerized by that and that alone.

"Are you sure it was okay?" Bodi asked anxiously, and Michael turned his head and murmured something. In the shadow cast by Bodi's face, Peter couldn't read his expression, but he could hear what Michael said.

"Yeah, it was good."

"I didn't hurt you, did I?"

"A little, at first," Michael admitted. He rolled to his side and put his hand up to Bodi's cheek and stroked a prominent cheekbone with his thumb. "But it felt really good after a while."

Bodi gnawed his lower lip anxiously. "But you didn't come."

"I will next time," Michael assured him, and Bodi slipped his hand between their bodies and started to stroke. Michael grunted and started to pump his hips slowly. "What're you doing?"

"Making sure there's a next time," Bodi said, and he was so serious. Peter wanted to poke Michael then, tell him that Bodi needed to hear words of reassurance, but Michael was lost in what Bodi was doing with his hand, and then Bodi started moving lower, lower, until he was low enough to take Michael's cock in his mouth.

Peter watched as Bodi serviced him completely, mouthing his cock, his balls, reaching back and fiddling between his legs until Michael knotted his hands in Bodi's blonding hair and groaned softly, coming, his eyes closed, his expression growing tight and fierce and then relaxing until he smiled lazily and pulled Bodi up to look at him through gratefully hooded eyes.

"Like there wouldn't be a next time," he said with a smile and then pulled Bodi in for a come-drenched kiss.

Peter didn't have to touch himself to come that time either.

He couldn't have come up with any justification for why he kept going to watch them after that, but he did. Not often. Not enough to arouse suspicion. Just enough to be able to feel an ownership of them, enough to feel like they were his, and to fall a little more in love with Bodi every time he did.

You could tell a lot about a man from the way he made love. Bodi was tender with Michael, patient, and Michael returned the favor. They cared for each other, tasted each other, were kind, funny, uninhibited, sexy. Peter might have missed the first time Bodi penetrated Michael, but he was there, watching, when Michael lubricated himself and begged Bodi to take him, actually used the word "fuck," and Peter got to see that wide-shouldered, lean and tanned body in action.

They did it face to face, one of Michael's legs cocked, foot flat on the ground, the other slung up over Bodi's shoulder, while Bodi moved so carefully, so smoothly, only Michael's soft gasp told Peter that he'd made it all the way in.

And the look on Michael's face as he'd looked up at his best friend, his only lover, was... luminous. Faithful. As though Bodi himself brought the dawn.

Bodi had started to move, and Michael's head had tilted back, his eyes had closed, and Bodi's hand on Michael's knee moved and tightened until Michael covered it with his own.

God, they'd been beautiful. Peter had come then too—but he'd cried afterwards, silently, almost happily, because they'd been so beautiful. It was okay this way. It was okay. Michael would take care of Bodi. That's all Peter wanted to do. If Michael could do it, then that would be fine. Michael could do anything better than Peter.

Peter could tell that the boys chafed when Michael was hurt. The Sunday after he got his cast off, Bodi paid Ashley Schlesinger thirty dollars to watch Juliet after church. He'd been honest—to an extent—and told his mother and Ashley and Juliet that he was going on a motorcycle ride with Michael, now that Michael could hold on. He'd been working late nights, trying to get the money for the business they'd been planning since they'd both graduated from high school. Since Michael had been out of commission for two months, Bodi had been tired and, well, sad. He mumbled to himself a lot, and his drawings, the silly little ones in the margins of his notebooks or even the larger, full-page ones that he did in his own room, when only Michael or Peter were there to see, had become muted. Even the things in his head had been sad.

Peter knew why—he'd been missing his soul mate. Michael had been either laid up or unable to come with Bodi to their secret place, to even spend time completely alone. Peter had started to do his homework in his room when Bodi came over, just to have an excuse to get out of the way and give them time to be together. More than once he'd seen his Aunt Aileen pull up in the driveway and had then run down the stairs with a purposeful clatter, just to warn them that she was there.

More than once he'd seen them jerk apart, their lips swollen, Bodi's neck chafed with razor stubble (since Michael had a beard that grew in if he wasn't careful). They would look at each other unhappily and go back to watching television, but their posture had been so close, their bodies had just throbbed with warmth.... Peter couldn't imagine how his aunt hadn't known about it. How could she be so blind? They were both so terribly in love.

But even though nobody really knew why they needed the time alone, everyone was okay with Bodi paying a babysitter. His sister was more and more difficult those days. They'd tried to put her in high school that year, because not only did she say she was lonely, but she'd been acting out more and more. The nurse the hospital sent told them flat out she was bored and she wanted a shot at a real life. After countless parent meetings and fighting the principal to the point where Bodi had to actually read educational code and cite it at the woman, they'd managed to get a special education class that would accommodate Juliet Kovacs.

It had lasted a week. She had no filter between what she thought and what she said. She told teachers they were full of shit, other students they were stupid, and the guys who picked on Peter that they deserved to have their dicks chopped off. (Peter actually agreed with that last one, but you didn't go around saying that shit.)

The school just assumed that Juliet would be happier at home—and the principal practically danced as she hand delivered her official "we can't accommodate this child" letter. It was horrible, because anyone who knew Juliet knew she took that rejection hard.

"And they say I'm the one who's retarded!" she sneered at the principal as the woman practically ran off their porch.

Peter was there that day, and he and Bodi looked at each other uneasily. She was not going to be happy at home anymore, and they had no place else to send her. She drew a lot of pictures of bloody knives and nooses in the following weeks, and no amount of Bodi's trips to Crescent City to see a doctor managed to come up with the combination of drugs that would help bring her out of that dangerous, hostile depression.

Peter watched her a couple of times during this period. He needed to call Bodi home once because she'd out-and-out attacked him, and Peter had ended up sitting on her chest and pinning her hands for ten minutes before she calmed down.

Bodi's lists became more and more wandering, and he'd lump motor oil in the same list as Velcro restraints and toilet paper. Even that absent look he'd get in his eyes when the world got to be one straw too heavy looked haunted. It was like even the places he went in his head for safety were coated in fear.

So when Bodi offered Ashley the money for two hours of uninterrupted time away, he'd needed the time—and so had his mother, who was going to spend the time with a church social group after service. Ashley was a pretty blonde girl from Michael and Bodi's graduating class who had been nice to both of them. Peter always suspected she had a little crush on Bodi, but true to form, Bodi never seemed to notice. When she asked if her boyfriend could help her babysit, Bodi had been a little hesitant at first. Warren had been in their graduating class, too, and his little brother had been the first kid to stuff Peter in a trashcan. But Ashley begged nicely, and Bodi finally relented. Juliet could still be dangerous, and Bodi warned Ashley, but finally he figured that if Juliet decided to attack, a big, strong guy like Warren would come in handy, right?

Well, sure. If Warren hadn't decided to use the lock on the outside of Juliet's room so he and Ashley could get busy while Juliet hung herself from a light fixture on the inside of the room, yeah. It would all have been fine.

It was stupid. So stupid. It was such a kid thing to do—so cliché, right? The babysitter was getting busy while the little kids were running around naked, putting peanut butter on the cat. Except Juliet wasn't a little kid. She was a sixteen-year-old emotionally disabled young adult, and she'd stolen the clothesline a month before, and she knew exactly what she was doing.

Peter hadn't gone to watch Michael and Bodi that time. He'd wanted to desperately, because those stolen moments watching them move together had felt like his time with Bodi, or as close to it as he'd ever get, but he hadn't. He'd opted to do homework instead. They'd needed the time together so badly, it had felt like these hours would be beyond private.

So when he heard the sirens down the block, he'd been reading in his room, and he'd been as able as anybody else to hop on his bicycle and go see what all the fuss was about.

When he saw the body being taken down the porch at Bodi's house, Juliet's blond hair was trailing out from under the sheet the MEs had pulled over her. His first thought was about telling Bodi. Oh God. Who was going to tell Bodi? It had to come from someone who loved him.

Bodi's mother was collapsed, sobbing, on the porch. Aileen and Joelle were holding her up between them. Warren and Ashley were holding hands tensely, talking to Larry Albrecht, the local police officer, and Warren looked up and caught Peter's eye just long enough for Peter to hear what he was saying.

"We didn't know. We'd just closed the door. We didn't know."

Warren sounded sorry then. Peter often thought that was the only reason he never hurt the man: because right then, he sounded sorry.

Peter heard the words, though, and whirled his bike around and took off. Somebody needed to tell Bodi.

He didn't realize that Warren was following him, driving slowly behind Peter as Peter pumped his bicycle up the winding hill toward the swimming hole where Michael and Bodi would be.

He cried most of the way there, a slide show of Juliet on her good days, of Bodi gently teaching her how to skip rope—again—or watching cartoons with her, playing in his mind. Oh God. Bodi was going to be destroyed. This would kill him. His little sister had been difficult. She'd sucked up all of their mother's time, she'd made his life hard, so hard, but he'd loved her, and somebody had to take care of her, and it might take more than Michael to make this loss right with him, it really might.

Peter made noise this time. He screamed Bodi's and Michael's names as he skidded his bike into the turnout that led to the swimming hole. He screamed them again after he dumped the bike next to Bodi's motorcycle, which was sitting there gleaming, perfect in the sun. He screamed their names as he ran, breathless, blubbering, down the embankment that protected them from view from the road, and into their clearing. By the time he got there, they'd pulled apart, stopped whatever they were doing, covered themselves with the sleeping bag, and were looking at him with wide-eyed fear.

"God, Bodi!" Peter panted, wiping his face on the shoulder of his T-shirt. "God. You gotta get dressed. You gotta get dressed and come into town. You gotta—"

"Oh Jesus—I always knew you were fuckin' faggots!" Warren yelled from the embankment as he slid down on his ass. "Your sister *died* so you could come be faggots in the woods!"

Peter turned around and watched with stunned eyes, and Warren ran back up the hill. The sound of the man's panicked skitter up the gravel embankment floated, surreal, like pollen, in the clear and quiet air. Peter hadn't even known Warren had been there, in the car or pulling into the turnout. He really didn't know that the guy had followed him on foot to Bodi and Michael's beyond private place. Slowly, he turned back to Bodi and Michael in time to watch Bodi's face crumple.

"Juliet?" he asked, his voice weak.

"I'm so sorry, Bodi," Peter whispered, but Bodi probably didn't hear the second, kinder voice telling him. He just heard that his sister was dead.

"Juliet?" Bodi asked again, and Michael leaned over and pulled Bodi into his arms while Bodi came unglued.

Peter sank to his ass in the forest dirt and hugged his knees. Oh God. Juliet. Yes, Juliet was the reason he'd come here. He knew, without a doubt, that by the time Warren got done shooting off his big mouth, no one would even remember Bodi's little sister's name in the shitstorm that was going to hit.

He was right.

ATONEMENT

BODI'S body felt so good as Peter held onto him on the back of the bike. The trees that covered the sheared sides of the mountain cast shade, and the day was sort of cool to begin with. Peter shivered and clutched Bodi closer, reassured by his animal warmth and by his sure control over the motorcycle as he took the curves of 122 with ease and skill.

The swimming hole was almost laughably close to Aileen's house, which was funny, since Peter hadn't been there in six years, and he was willing to bet that Bodi hadn't either. It looked mostly the same. A road crew had come by the year before and shored up the curb and fixed up guardrail to the turnout where Bodi parked the bike, but there was a gap in the rail, and that's what they walked through. Bodi had packed a bedroll on the back and an ice chest under that, with a small duffel with clothes and toiletries on the top. It had all been anchored to the bitch bar with the extra helmet, and they hauled Bodi's camping shit with them as they half walked, half skidded down the embankment to the little clearing above the river.

They didn't say much as Bodi unrolled his bag and the soft egg crate foam under it, under the same big-boled redwood tree he and Michael had huddled under during all those stolen moments making love. Peter helped him string the ice chest up because there was a very real threat of bears if you weren't careful. Bodi was going to use his duffel bag for a pillow, which sounded as uncomfortable as hell to Peter but was still better than taking a room out from Daisy's only hotel. The place was well known as a fleabag trap for tourists travelling too late to get to the ocean, as well as a haven for men fighting with their wives.

When they were done with setting up camp, Peter stalked restlessly from one corner of the clearing to the next. He spent a moment in the sunny corner of it, the one he and Michael had been standing in on that first day when Bodi stripped to the skin and titillated them both. He stood there and looked out at the rock, seeing Bodi as he had been, lean, tan, confident. He'd still been Bodi, still more of the wind in long grasses and the sea and high tide than of the earth, but he'd been whole.

Restlessly Peter turned around, seeking and finding his little corner of brush suspended between two trees, and wondered if he was too grown to hide behind it these days. He went to the big tree first—it had grown proportionally bigger, which served as sort of a mindfuck for a minute, because it made him think he was thirteen again, but the brush itself hadn't grown, so he was reassured.

Bodi's voice behind him was... surprising. Low. Harsh. Intimate.

"You knew where we'd be," he said, and Peter closed his eyes. Yeah. Michael never had put that together.

"I knew," he said softly, leaning against the tree, pushing his cheek against the rough bark. It was a Joshua pine with the gray bark that looked like jigsaw puzzle pieces as the outer layer flaked off. It smelled like cookies, and Peter closed his eyes and breathed deeper.

"How long?" Bodi asked, and now he was right behind Peter, holding himself just far enough away that their bodies didn't touch.

"Since I was thirteen."

Peter felt Bodi's exhalation ruffle the longish hair at the back of his neck. "God, Peter. Why didn't you ever say anything?"

Peter kept his eyes closed, imagined what would happen if Bodi just hugged him, let go against him, kissed the back of his neck, rubbed up against his backside. God, all these years, knowing how sex worked, knowing who he wanted to have it with, and it was now just far enough away to hurt.

"Because you were with Michael, and he was taking care of you." Behind his eyes, Peter could see his cousin—those big dark eyes, that laughing mouth. Michael had been able to do anything: confront bullies, stand up to Aileen for Peter, take care of Bodi. God, Michael could do anything.

"Fucking wonderful," Bodi snapped. Peter felt him step back, the air between them charging with intimate anger instead of intimate longing. "You just... six years? I mean... you thought he was taking care of me?"

Peter turned his body slightly so he could look over his shoulder. "What do you want me to say, Bodi? I loved you. I loved you since... God, since I met you."

"So you just watched us? Doing that shit, that nasty—"

"Shut up!" Peter snarled, furious. "It was beautiful. Hell yes, I watched. Jesus, Bodi—it was first time I knew being gay wasn't a bad thing! Those fuckers at school—they could say fucking anything they wanted, but I *saw* you. You were fucking beautiful, you and Michael. And you cared for one another, and it was *gorgeous.* Don't you make that bad!"

Bodi's face was taut, the flesh drawn back until his cheekbones threatened to rip out of the skin. "That time...." He closed his eyes and swallowed. "That time took away everything I loved!"

Peter grabbed his shoulder and shook it. "Your time with Michael didn't do that," he snapped. "The town did. God, Bodi— this is when you get to be mad. But don't be mad that you had a lover—be mad that they killed the love!"

Bodi grabbed both his shoulders and whirled him completely around so they were face to face. "You think I'm mad at them? I'm not mad at them. We knew who they were! We knew what we were dealing with. But we kept saying, you know? We kept saying, as long as we were together, we could beat them... as long as we were together, it would be okay. But... God, I don't even know what your aunt said to him. One minute we were going to go make a future together, alone but just us, and the next... the next, he dropped me off in Arcata and just fucking disappeared. Just that fucking letter and his orders...." Bodi's voice was flaking, growing brittle, and with every word, another splinter flew off and flayed Peter's heart.

"Then be mad at *him!*" Peter said. He squeezed Bodi's shoulder. "Be mad at him, Bodi. Be mad at *somebody,* just... just let it out, man... just—"

"Let it out? *Let it out?*" Bodi's hands clenched in front of him, held so tight they were shaking. "You don't want me to let it out—it's... God, Peter, it's so ugly." And finally, the tears, flooding over his mouth, flooding his broken voice. "It's ugly and I hate it... it's... it's turning my brain to red, man, I can't... I can't hardly sit in my own skin anymore, it's all so much hate—" He crumpled then, would have fallen to the ground like refuse, but Peter grabbed his face, mindless of the tears and the runny nose, and kissed him, hard.

Anger. It was all anger. Bodi forced him back against the tree and savaged him, mashed his lips against Peter's teeth so tight Peter thought his lips would bleed, and Peter didn't care because it was in him too. He kissed back, his hand pushed hard against the back of Bodi's head, knotted cruelly to keep Bodi in place, and Bodi didn't fight him, welcomed him in fact, pinning his shoulders there against the tree, rutting his groin up against Peter's. They were both suddenly, painfully aroused.

Peter bucked forward against him and groaned, while Bodi fumbled briefly with Peter's jeans, shoving them down to his knees without subtlety or grace. That quickly, he had Peter's erection in his fist and was pumping, strong enough to hurt, but Peter wanted the pain. He'd done this, he thought through the haze of lust. He'd done this. Bodi needed pain, right? Well, he could have Peter's. Peter had stolen from him and Michael, had taken the beauty of those secret hours and kept it in his heart. Bodi needed it back, and Peter would give it to him any way he needed it. It was all he had.

Peter thrust into Bodi's fist and fumbled with Bodi's fly. He thrust his hand into Bodi's pants, grasping him too. He was fully erect, his foreskin retracted, and Peter stroked, pulling the foreskin over the crown and back, and Bodi's howl into his shoulder bordered on a scream of pain. Peter slackened his grip, and Bodi whispered harshly.

"No... no... hard. I got no gentleness in me, Petey, I got nothin' but hate...."

Peter shoved his pants down then, jerked away from Bodi, and leaned against the tree, thrusting his bare ass in the air. He took two fingers, sucked them in his mouth, and spit on them, harsh and thick and wet, because this was the worst way. He'd read about it and nobody did this and liked it, but that didn't stop him from reaching his hand around to his asshole and shoving them in, gasping with the sudden intrusion, the pain, the burn, even more when he scissored his fingers outward, stretching as wide as he could.

Bodi bent over him, leaned over his back, his chest covering Peter's shoulders, his cock pressed up against Peter's ass cheek as he breathed harshly in Peter's ear. "You want this, Petey? It's gonna hurt. I can't make this good. I can't make it sweet... I don't got that in me. Not today."

"Shut up and do it," Peter snapped, the burn and the cold of his ass out there in the spring air deflating his erection but not his lust, not his hatred or his pain. He wanted this. *Needed* it. If the only way he could have Bodi Kovacs in his body was like this, pissed off and raw, then that's what he'd take.

Bodi leaned back for a moment and Peter heard him spit several times, felt the wet on his hole, and readied himself inside, relaxing. When Bodi pushed his cock against Peter's entrance, he pushed out against it, engulfing Bodi's crown in one shove. Peter cried out, burying his face in his shoulder, bumping his sore nose and then biting his upper arm hard enough to bruise, because *God*, did it hurt. Not enough spit in the world to make that fit easy, but it was there, and his body was shaking and there was a rim of fire in his vision as his brain filled with that stretchy burn. Bodi slid, buried deeply inside his body, their flesh made one.

Bodi grunted, thrust further, and Peter dragged a sweating hand through his hair and weathered the pain. Finally, finally, Bodi was all the way inside, and he wrapped his hands around Peter's shoulders and hid his face against Peter's neck. "I'm sorry," he grunted. "I'm sorry. I'm sorry."

"Don't be sorry," Peter said, aware that his knees were trembling, aware that he was crying, though from the pain in his body or the pain in his heart, he couldn't tell. "Don't be sorry. Just fuck me, Bodi. Just do it, man. Fuck me. Use me. You're due."

Bodi pulled back then, and Peter shuddered in relief, but too soon, because Bodi was thrusting again, and Peter's groan ripped out from his belly. Again, and again, and again, and that rim of fire faded, turned gold, started to shine, and Peter's cock began to stir in the cool air. He was sweating, the sweat dripping into his eyes and stinging, but still, oh my God, they were doing it, they were doing it, he was giving something that Bodi needed and it was filling him, filling him up, taking away the empty that he'd fought for so long.

Bodi was moving faster now, and Peter found he was bucking back, wanting it, wanting the violence and the edge of the next thrust. One of Bodi's hands was gripping his shoulder hard enough to leave bruises and the other was splayed on his lower back, forcing him to arch his spine, thrust his ass out, beg for it, and oh God, he did, he wanted it, wanted Bodi to use him, take him, cleanse him of everything, the hate, the anger, the pain, leaving only room for Bodi, the real Bodi, the beautiful boy with the smile that Peter would live for, the man who should have been.

Bodi's thrusts increased, grew more frenzied, and Peter's cock bobbed painfully, smacking against his thigh as Bodi gave one final lunge into Peter's body and screamed release into the still mountain air. Peter felt Bodi's come spurting inside him, the heat and the salt stinging as it ran out, and he let out a needing sound. He wasn't done yet. Dammit... his body still needed, still wanted, with all of that use. Bodi wrapped his arms around Peter's waist and buried his face in Peter's neck again, whispering, "I'm sorry, I'm sorry, I'm sorry," and Peter turned in his embrace and clenched Bodi's skinny body next to his own, rutting up against him instinctively. He gasped, his vision going dark, and his climax spurted between them, making their skin slick and sticky, and still, Bodi's face was buried in his neck, and the litany never stopped.

"I'm sorry, I'm sorry, I'm sorry...."

And Peter gave him back the words that should have been Bodi's from the beginning. "I'm sorry, I'm sorry, I'm so sorry...."

Bodi sobbed, broke down, disintegrated, losing himself in grief and remorse. Peter kept his arms wrapped around those wide shoulders, anchoring Bodi to the present, because the past could not be borne.

WARREN made it to town long before the three of them. Bodi and Michael had dressed quickly, and Peter pretended along with them that nothing had happened in that clearing beyond two boys swimming, even though it was fall and too late for the water to be even tolerable.

Bodi kept asking for details, and Peter had none. "I don't know, Bodi," he said again and again. "I just know she's dead."

"But how?" Bodi snapped, and Michael turned to him, pulled him close, gentled him.

"We'll find out, okay? We'll find out, Bodi. You still have me, okay? You still have us."

It worked. Bodi managed to pilot the motorcycle, and Peter followed way behind on his bicycle, careening down the hill like cars coming up the road didn't exist.

By the time he got there, the nature of the tragedy had changed completely, and Peter was left gasping with the shock.

"So what were you two doing in the woods again?" Officer Albrecht was saying, and Michael's face was as dark as his complexion would let it be. Bodi's eyes were unfocused and elsewhere. Peter knew that look. Bodi had effectively checked out. As Peter skidded his bike into Bodi's front yard, he watched Bodi's lips move, and as he drew near, he could hear him mumble.

"Talk to the coroner, get the death certificate, talk to the insurance agent, get the death benefits, Mom doesn't know what they are, arrange the funeral, she liked daisies, hated roses, wanted Sheryl Crow's 'Lifetimes' played at her funeral, wanted cremation, told me, told me, knew she was leaving, damn her...."

Officer Albrecht didn't even look at him. Instead, he concentrated all his venom on Michael, and Michael, who had been loved on the football team and celebrated when he graduated at the top of the class, Michael, whom everybody trusted to watch their children and who had known nothing but the town's adulation and his mother's unswerving devotion for his entire life...

Michael was breaking.

"What does it matter what we were doing?" he asked, and to Peter it sounded like he'd said it more than once. "What happened to his sister? He paid good money—"

"Yes, but why?"

"He needed a break," Peter said, because Michael's throat was flushing and he was near tears. Bodi was clutching at his hand, and Michael wasn't returning the clasp, and Peter wanted to be brave and protect them both.

Officer Albrecht looked over his shoulder at Peter and turned away in dismissal, bending his focus back on Michael. "So where did you go? Why did Mr. Kovacs here need a break?"

"He was exhausted," Peter said, but his voice wasn't strong, it wasn't even heard. "He was exhausted and so worried. Why can't you leave him alone?"

At that moment there was a scream from the porch, and Peter looked beyond Bodi and Michael and saw Bodi's mother running across her yard to throw herself bodily at Bodi, screaming and kicking and biting and scratching. Officer Albrecht just let her— Michael and Peter pulled her off, and by the time they got her situated across the yard, Bodi had simply sat down in his front yard, weeping silently into his knees.

The rest of the day—God. Peter only saw bits and pieces of it, heard angry voices, snide insinuations, terrible, painful names from adults that Peter had only heard before from children. At the end of the day, Michael took his mother's car while she screamed at him to get his faggot ass back on her lawn, because she didn't raise him this way. He and Bodi had disappeared, and in the end, Bodi didn't get to do any of the planning for his sister's funeral. Michael just took him away, apparently used all that money that they had worked for and set him up in Arcata, and Bodi, who had clung to Michael all through school, clung to his hand so tightly that day when he'd needed somebody the most, had been left alone.

Michael returned two days later, without a word.

When Aileen had tried to confront him about it, he said, "Mom, his sister died—doesn't anyone remember that?"

"But what you two were doing out there in the woods—"

"Was our business!"

"But it wasn't natural!"

"But it was *our* business! We could have done that for the rest of our lives, and nobody would have known. Doesn't anybody care that this is the last thing we should be worrying about?"

"Just tell me that it's done! You and that boy ain't gonna—"

"No! I won't tell you that!"

"Tell me that or I'll tell the world I ain't got no son! I'd rather you were dead than be a faggot!"

Peter's breath died in his throat. He'd been lurking on top of the stairs, and he watched all the color drain from Michael's face. He couldn't see Aileen, she had her back to him, but Michael—oh God. Peter should have known. They all should have known. That moment right there—that catalyzed everything: Michael's enlistment two days later, the way he shipped out without a word. Michael stepped on a land mine that day, in the middle of his kitchen, with the mother he thought had at least loved him, even if she'd never loved Peter.

"Okay," Michael said softly. He walked up the stairs blindly, past Peter without even so much as a hand on his shoulder. Peter watched him go into his room and had run outside, jumped on his bike, and ridden back to the swimming hole. It had been deserted— no lovers in the shadows, no playful children in the water. Just the quiet of the rushing river and the cobalt of the sky. Peter had leaned against the tree—Bodi and Michael's tree—and he'd cried for all of them, for Juliet, who was dead, and for Michael, whose eyes had just died, and for Bodi, who was far away from comfort and from love and who Peter was not sure would ever, ever come back.

THE same noises were here that had been there that day, but the sky was lighter, not the deep cobalt of autumn, and Peter could feel the heartblood of the earth stirring in the spring air. He and Bodi were kneeling in the leaf mold, naked and dripping in come, and Bodi was sobbing in his arms.

Peter gentled him, shushed him, stroked his brown/blond hair back from his face, and whispered that it was all right. He was drenched in sweat, cooling in the spring shade, and Bodi was a hot, salty mess against his chest and his shoulder. Peter wouldn't have moved him for the world.

Finally Bodi's sobs eased and he pulled back, looking embarrassed.

"I'm sorry," he whispered one more time and finished on a laugh as he wiped his face on the long-sleeved T-shirt he'd worn under his denim jacket.

"Not as sorry as I am," Peter told him, reaching out to cup his heated face.

Bodi nodded and looked over his shoulder. "I'm going swimming," he said out of the blue. "I don't give a shit how cold it is. I've got to...."

He stood up then and started stripping, and Peter followed, picking Bodi's clothes up off the forest floor so he could leave them on Bodi's bedroll. After he stripped off his own T-shirt and shook the leaves and pine needles out of his jeans and underwear, he turned and watched as Bodi, naked and skinny, pale in the sunshine, climbed to the top of the granite boulder so he could jump into the deep pool that formed in the bend of the river.

He looked proud and beautiful, young and unafraid, and he whooped as he leaped and seemed to hang suspended for a minute under the spring sun.

SUNSHINE

THE water was chill to the point of shock, and Peter fought not to panic as it closed over his head. He kicked clear to the surface, fighting the mild current, and tried to catch his breath. By the time he'd thrown his hair out of his eyes and looked up, Bodi was standing on the shore, shivering, and Peter thought he'd join him. There was a granite shelf near the beach, and he swam until he could feel that under the sand and the murk of the bottom. Once his feet touched, he walked up the side.

Bodi held out a hand for him to make that final step up to the rock that served as a ledge, and Peter took it, surprised when Bodi pulled him, wet and shivering, into his arms.

They stood for a moment, bodies naked and touching, skin on skin in the sun, and Peter found he was melting into Bodi's embrace like it was going to last. He shivered and burrowed deeper, careful of his nose, which was aching with the cold. Oh God, did he want it to last.

Bodi's arms grew tighter, and then he pulled away. "Here, let's get the bag in the sun and warm up," he muttered. "The next time I want my balls to shrivel up and disappear, I'll just jump off an airplane naked and skip the part where I almost drown."

Peter snickered and walked to the clearing and helped Bodi move the bag—clothes on top and all—to the corner of the meadow that sat in the sun. They opened the bag up and sat down on it, still naked, and Peter leaned back on his elbows and tilted his head into the sun and let the heat sink into his chilled skin. For a moment, sadness, anger, hurt—all those things disappeared, and it was just the air on his body and the peace and the sound of the river.

There was movement, chilled skin close enough to touch his own, and a shadow over his face. He opened one eye, and there was Bodi, close enough that kissing was a possibility, far enough to look in his eyes comfortably as he spoke.

"I... I'm sorry," he said, and Peter sighed.

"Don't be." He brought a hand up and cupped the side of Bodi's face.

"It was your first time, Petey. I... if it was going to be me, it should have been...." Bodi closed his eyes then and lowered his head, allowing his lips to touch Peter's. "Sweeter," he whispered. "It should have been sweeter."

Peter closed his eyes, too, seeing the red throb of the sun behind them but not caring. Bodi brushed his lips again, and Peter opened his mouth and pushed his hand from Bodi's cheek to the back of his head. Their kiss deepened, and Peter closed his eyes tighter, to trap Bodi there, mouth moving on his, hand moving against his chest and his abdomen, the sensitive skin of his upper thigh.

Bodi pulled back for a minute, panting, and Peter traced his closed, swollen lips with a pointed tongue. "You want me to know sweetness?" he breathed, and Bodi grunted, questioning. "Then teach me sweetness."

"Peter, I—"

Peter rubbed his lips on the corner of Bodi's mouth, across his cheek, to the cup of his ear. "Don't tell me you can't," he whispered. "Don't tell me you don't have it in you." He threaded his fingers down through Bodi's hair and then moved his palm until it was flat against Bodi's chest. "It's in you, Bodi. You've got all that bullshit behind you, I know, but your heart still isn't anything but sweet."

Bodi's hand came up, trapped Peter's hand against his chest, and he dragged his lips down Peter's jaw to the point of his chin.

"Petey, I'm broken," he whispered, and Peter whimpered. His skin was heating with arousal, and Bodi was *right there.*

93

"Then let me fix you." Peter shifted backward, slowly so his head didn't thunk on the ground beneath the sleeping bag. Bodi leaned over him, covering him with his shoulders, keeping him safe.

"You think this'll do it?" Bodi asked, but he was stroking Peter's chest, kissing Peter's temple, falling into the spell of heating skin and sunshine.

"I think it's a start," Peter vowed, and he turned his head, raised his lips, captured Bodi's mouth even from the bottom. Bodi allowed himself to be captured, and they took each other, tangled their tongues, tasted each other, and Peter placed faith in Bodi like he hadn't placed faith in anyone but Michael.

Bodi didn't let him down.

Suddenly Bodi let Peter know he'd done this before. He kissed hard, cupped Peter's jaw in his finger and thumb, and forced his mouth open wider, and Peter let him, opening his arms, welcoming Bodi's body on top of his. The kiss was long, dominating, wet, and by the time Bodi left his mouth to work his way down Peter's chest, Peter was painfully aroused. Bodi paused at his chest and licked a drop of sweat from the middle of his pecs. He looked down for a moment and then grinned up at Peter.

"You know, this isn't small potatoes, Petey. This thing… this thing here is pretty impressive."

Peter grinned. "I was hoping you'd notice someday."

Bodi looked thoughtful for a moment before taking one of Peter's nipples in his mouth and suckling it until Peter squirmed and fisted his hair. Peter groaned, and Bodi let it pop out of his mouth with a smack.

"I was noticing then," he said softly before moving to Peter's other nipple, and Peter's body was thrumming with need, but his heart….

"Yeah?" he gasped, and Bodi nibbled on the sensitive end of Peter's nipple until Peter grunted and wiggled some more. "C'mon, Bodi, gimme something here…."

Bodi looked up then, pierced Peter past the center of his soul with those blue eyes. "You were always more than Michael's cousin to me, Peter," he said. "I don't know if we would have been anything six years ago, but two years ago, after Michael walked away from me, you were the first person I thought of." He lowered his gaze then, kissed Peter's ribs, worked his way down to Peter's stomach, and for a moment Peter's desire faded. Peter had been the first person Bodi had thought of, but Peter had been here, locked in this town by a wish for a man who had apparently left him without a backward glance.

But Bodi hadn't stopped kissing, and his mouth found the crown of Peter's cock, and Peter shuddered, groaned, and doubled up, catching his breath as he tried desperately not to come this soon. This *was* his first time, Bodi *was* his first lover, and all of those furtive moments under a begrudged roof paled in comparison to this moment witnessed by God, under the depthless blue of the spring sky.

"No," he begged, and Bodi kept him in a stroking fist and looked up, smiling kindly from his perch on Peter's thigh.

"It's okay, Petey. Let go. I've gotcha this time, I swear."

He punctuated this by taking Peter's crown in his mouth again, while stroking firmly, and Peter couldn't help it, couldn't make it last. He gasped and closed his eyes as his world exploded in red and gold and he spurted hard, again and again, into Bodi's working mouth.

He shuddered for quite some time afterward, and Bodi kept milking him, kept sucking, kept stroking; he even squeezed Peter's balls and made him shudder and shudder again. When Peter finally couldn't take it anymore, his cock limp and tender and his body trembling from coming so long and so hard, he knotted his fingers in Bodi's hair and tugged. Bodi came up, wiping his mouth with the back of his hand and resting his cheek on Peter's shoulder.

"Sorry," Peter mumbled. "That was over really quick."

Bodi's smile was pure as the sunshine that warmed their bodies. "No, Petey—it was great. It's been a long time since someone let me do that, trusted me like that. It felt good."

Peter made a noncommittal sound and stroked the hair back from Bodi's face. "Are you ready?" he asked into the quiet. "To tell me?"

Bodi hmmed into Peter's shoulder. "We'll have to get dressed in a few," he apologized, and Peter's disappointment was acute. Then Bodi rescued him from that. "We'll burn if we stay naked in the sun, and it's too cold to sit in the shade and talk."

His arm was sprawled across Peter's chest, and Peter stroked it, thinking about the track marks on the inside. "You don't want to do this naked," he said softly, and Bodi grunted.

"You were always so smart," he said. "You'd just watch us— just observe—but you could wrench on a bike just by watching what we did. Michael wanted you to be in school so bad."

"I will be," Peter told him, not wanting to close his eyes. Bodi in his arms was too much of a miracle. "It's waiting."

"What are you going to do?" Bodi asked, and Peter made sure he was looking in Bodi's eyes when he answered.

"I'm going to learn business and bookkeeping so I can help you in the shop."

Bodi sat up suddenly. "That's not what Michael wanted," he said, his voice breaking with the torsion between hope and refusal.

Peter sat up and wrapped his arms around his knees. It wasn't a no. "Michael's not here," he said. "And even if he was still alive, he left you. You're fair game. If I'd known he'd left you in the first place, I would have already made you mine."

Bodi shook his head. "Better things, Petey. Better people. You were supposed to shoot for the moon."

He stood up then and grabbed his briefs from the pile of clothes next to Peter and struggled to put them on. He had his foot through one leg and was struggling for balance when Peter caught a flailing hand and said, "Lean on me, Bodi. The tides won't stop because I left the moon in the sky and got you instead."

Bodi sighed, put the hand on Peter's shoulder, and pulled his underwear up, then reached for the brown T-shirt—a nice color on him, actually—and pulled it on. Finally, he put on the denim jacket he'd taken off when they'd been hauling the ice chest up into the tree.

He used Peter to balance again for his jeans, and Peter sat and watched him before he put his own clothes on. There was power, he thought, in being naked, in being sure, when your opponent/soul mate was struggling to put on his clothes for armor.

Finally Bodi was dressed, and Peter got up and pulled on his boxers, jeans, and T-shirt before he and Bodi moved the sleeping bag back into the shade. Peter sat down and shivered, and Bodi sat down and wrapped an arm over his shoulder, and they both leaned back against the big redwood tree that Michael and Bodi had made love under. The fact that he and Bodi had now made love twice, and not once had it been under this tree, made Peter feel good somehow. It was ownership, and he was good with that.

"So…," Peter said leadingly, turning his head to catch the scent of his skin. Something about Bodi—Peter couldn't imagine him smelling like shampoo or cologne. He smelled like clean river right now, and Peter wanted to fill his lungs with that, wanted to breathe it forever.

"So…," Bodi echoed and then sighed. "So he came back. Two years ago. Showed up after his second tour, knocked on my door… fucked me stupid for about two weeks." Bodi laughed humorlessly. "They were really good weeks," he apologized. "We didn't… we didn't talk about anything. It was like he'd never been gone, like my sister never died. He helped me in the shop, and we just…."

"Just were," Peter filled in, thinking that was how he'd always imagined them when he was a kid.

"Yeah. We just were. But... but all that other shit had happened. And I didn't realize he was using the whole time—that he'd picked it up in the army, he'd been shooting between his toes."

Peter made a sound of actual loss and felt Bodi's hand in his hair, soothing, apologizing, everything.

"And then I woke up one night and there he was. On my damned couch, his little kit out, trying to find a vein. And then he told me to try it, because when you tried it, all that shit—everything we were pretending didn't happen, right? My sister here in a grave I ain't never seen, the whole town telling us it was our fault just for... just for being us? That went the fuck away."

There were tears in Bodi's voice then. Peter sat up, wiggled, took Bodi in his arms and forced *his* head on Peter's chest, and he went. Because someone should have taken him to their heart a long time ago. Because Michael should have, but apparently Michael had been just as broken as Bodi, except worse, because he dragged Bodi down into that brokenness and... and what? Left him there?

"Did it work?" Peter asked after they'd wordlessly resituated so Peter could just hold him while he continued the story.

"Oh yeah," Bodi said fervently. "It was awesome. But... I mean, I know people who can do that shit and be all functional like, you know, like I do pot, where it's for after hours only. Your cousin was one, because he'd been doing it for *years*, and I don't think he'd been busted, probably not even when...." He didn't finish that sentence, and Peter didn't want him to. Peter was pissed at Michael—it was easier to be pissed when Michael was alive, after having dragged Bodi down to hell, and not dead, with so much left to answer for.

"So you couldn't?" Peter prompted, because he needed to know.

"Not the hard stuff," Bodi sighed. "Not smack. No." He half laughed. "And it's hard to obtain up here too. I mean pot— *everybody's* got some in their basement, but smack? That shit's expensive! Anyway, it took me about a month before the shop was about ready to go bust, and Shawn caught me using in the bathroom one day, and…." Bodi shook his head. "I still don't know what happened. One minute I had my kit out and I was about to get high, and the next I had this big cut on my forehead and my needles and my stash—that was fucking gone. Shawn put me in the car and I thought we were going to go fix the big cut on my forehead, and I woke up in rehab." Bodi's crossed eyes were mildly indignant. "I don't even know how to get to that place now, Peter. She just *drove* me there and took over the business for a month. And Michael had been living with me, right? And, like, my second day in rehab—I still had a bandage on my head and everything, was still going through withdrawals…." Bodi sat up and looked at Peter seriously then. "Peter, don't ever do smack. Quitting it sucks. I mean… *sucks*. It's so bad. I thought having my sister die would hurt worse than anything I could imagine, and it does… but… but smack is something you miss *inside your skin*, and it's awful. Don't ever do it, okay? You gotta promise me."

Peter nodded soberly. "I promise, Bodi." *I promise I'll take such good care of you that you and me, we'll never need to do drugs again, not pot, not smack, and beer only 'cause it tastes good.*

"Promise." Bodi nodded again, and Peter nodded back.

"Swear. What did Michael say when he came to visit?"

Bodi sighed and sort of drooped. "He said good-bye."

Peter grunted and went to pull him back, but Bodi shrugged him off. Instead of leaning on Peter, he stood up and took a few steps off the sleeping bag, until his bare feet were on the forest floor.

"Was that all?"

"No, it wasn't all." Bodi had crossed his arms in front of him and was starting to shiver. "He said that he must not have loved me, because you didn't just fuck up the people you loved. He said that I'd be better off without him and that I'd been doing great and he'd been the mess, and he should have left me like that." Bodi laughed without humor. "He said he'd left Shawn some money to fix up the business and that I needed to keep that going, because that had been our dream and he needed to know I was living that." Bodi looked down and then finished. "He said... he *begged* me not to tell you, and he said he was re-upping for another tour.

"I said he needed to be safe, and that was the one promise he made. I figure, he broke that, then I'd break my promise not to tell you, because... because...."

Oh shit... he was disintegrating, dissolving, coming apart again, and Peter needed to be there, for once *someone* needed to be there to catch Bodi as he fell.

Peter was up and wrapping his arms around Bodi before one more painful word could happen, and Bodi was crying, crying like he hadn't cried when his sister had died, and Peter was crying with him, because this was *Michael* Bodi was crying about, and Michael had hurt and Michael had broken and he hadn't let them fix him, and now he would never be fixed, and they'd always be just a little bit broken in the part of their souls where he'd left the Michael-shaped hole.

SHINING UP THE CHROME

WHEN the shadows started lengthening and the sun got narrower on the horizon, they went back. They had to. They had a job to do.

Bodi rolled up his bag and stowed it in the tree with his clothes, saying he figured he'd had his shower for the day, and they walked up to the turnoff to get on the bike so they could go back and finish what they'd started.

Peter was swinging his foot over the back of the bike, grateful for the room he had now that Bodi's luggage was elsewhere, when he winced. His backside was tender—there was no escaping it.

Bodi was still standing by the bike and saw it. He waited until Peter was seated on the bike, and cupped Peter's cheek, bringing his face close. "I'm sorry," he said firmly. "Don't tell me I can't be, little brother. It's not supposed to hurt like that, I—" He grimaced.

Peter caught his hand, pulled it back, kissed the palm. "You're forgiven," he said, that simply. "I forgave you before you did it, Bodi. I hope that's okay."

Bodi swallowed—Peter watched his throat work for a moment. "That's terrifying," he said. "Nothing's scarier than unconditional love."

After a life like Bodi's? Yeah. You were always waiting for strings, weren't you?

The chill of evening in the mountains was starting to set in, and after Bodi pulled up to the garage, Peter told him he was going inside for some old sweatshirts. Michael had some he'd used for working on cars, and Peter knew just where he kept them.

Bodi nodded and practically charged inside the garage. Peter could tell that after the emotion of the day, Bodi wanted his happy place, the place where everything made sense. Peter couldn't blame him even a little.

He slid into the kitchen and up the stairs without even looking for Aileen—he was too intent on his one goal: getting in and out of Michael's room without thinking much about how Michael was never going to be in it again.

Aileen was in there, stripping the bed of sheets. There were several boxes filled with the clothes Michael had left behind.

Peter froze with his hand on the doorframe, making a quick decision to use some of his own old sweatshirts and ruin them with grease. He hadn't worked on a car more than to gap the plugs and change the oil since high school and didn't have the grease-stained clothes that Michael had.

"You win," Aileen said, her voice flat. Peter looked around the room, saw that she'd taken down all of Michael's posters featuring Harleys and football stars, all of his sports trophies, all of his academic awards—they were all dumped in a box, not even stacked, and Peter wondered exactly what it was he was supposed to have won.

"What happened?"

"Mail came," she said shortly. "I put it on your dresser."

"Thank you," Peter said, his throat dry. Apparently there were some letters that hadn't made it to his dresser before.

"He picked you," she muttered. "I don't understand…." She turned to Peter, honest anguish on her face. "He was the best baby. He was so sweet. His daddy was gone, and it was just me, and I worked, and I'd come home and he'd climb on my lap and just…." She swallowed, and for a moment, Peter saw a young mother, exhausted, frazzled, and then, oddly, comforted. "He'd just put his hands on either side of my face and say, 'It's okay, Mommy. Let me make you a sandwich.' And then he would. He'd make me a peanut butter sandwich and…." She shook her head. "I thought it would just be the two of us. I thought that's all we would ever need. And then… then you came. And he was so excited." She looked at him, and for the first time he could ever remember, she didn't seem to see a burden or a duty—she saw *him.* "You just... just watched us all. You didn't smile, you didn't play. I thought you'd need a mother, but you didn't seem to want anything. But Michael—Michael would get you a sandwich and I could see it. The sun just rose with him, and you didn't need me at all. And so I didn't have you, and Michael—he... he would rather spend time with you and that Kovacs boy, and I lost him. And he was all I had."

Peter blinked for a moment, and for a moment, his anger surged back. *You never offered me anything but charity!* But then, he'd been ten—how would he have known?

"I didn't trust mothers," he said gruffly. It was true. "Mine left me, and even if I know she meant it for the best, I didn't trust another mother. But I'd never had a brother."

Aileen nodded, and for the first time in maybe Peter's whole life, he saw a sort of acceptance for him on her face. "Why'd he leave?" she asked. "He didn't just leave me. He left you too, and that other boy. Why'd he leave?"

Peter closed his eyes and wondered if he should tell the truth, and then he opened them and realized that he was planning on putting Daisy in his rearview too. Aileen truly *would* be alone, and maybe the truth would be the only thing she would have.

"Just because he was in love with Bodi didn't mean he didn't love you too," he said and almost backed up from the fire in her eyes. "It didn't mean you couldn't break his heart."

"Do you really hate me that much, Peter?" she asked, her voice crumbling. She held Michael's old sheets in one hand and wiped her cheeks with the back of the other. The sunlight streaming through Michael's window seemed to erase the lines in her face, washed over the grays in her blonde hair, illumined her light-brown eyelashes, showing eyes that, while red-rimmed with grief, had once been a pretty blue.

"You hated me before you even knew me," Peter said, and he was resigned and sad. God, so much to be angry about—but it was too hard to be angry when she was like this, helpless, blind, maybe finally seeing what she'd done.

"I did not!" She was honestly surprised.

"Aunt Aileen, I came home from school when I was twelve years old, and I was in tears 'cause the other kids called me a faggot. You remember that?"

"Yeah," Aileen said, looking away.

"You remember what you said?"

She sighed like this was inevitable. "I said 'You don't wanna hear it, stop being one.'"

"You remember what Michael said?"

Aileen shook her head. "No," she murmured.

"No—you left the room at that point. He said, 'They're all assholes. Let's go get ice cream.' And then he and Bodi spent the next two years beating them up whenever they got out of hand. Even before I knew they were together, I knew they didn't give a shit what I was. You want to know what Michael wanted from you? He wanted the same thing I did. When the world turned against him, he wanted you to have his back. You didn't. Without you, he didn't feel like he could have anybody's back, Aunt Aileen. It's why he left Daisy, and Bodi, and…." He swallowed, still angry, but said it anyway. "And me."

Aileen looked away. "What he and Bodi were doing—"

"Was none of anyone's goddamned business," Peter snapped, because the whine in her voice, the self-righteous whine, sparked his anger all over again.

"But God said—"

"What? To turn your back on your baby boy? That it was better to be dead than to be a fag? Well, congratulations, Aunt Aileen. You got your wish. Your baby boy is dead. But you know what the real tragedy is? The real tragedy is that the boy you loved? The one who made you sandwiches and tried to comfort you and who thought he could take care of the people he loved? *That* boy died six years ago, and nobody in this fucking town cared to see it."

He'd made her cry harder, and he couldn't comfort her. He couldn't. God, he felt twisted inside. Just a few moments ago he'd touched Bodi's hand with his own, said he'd be right back, and he felt like there might be peace waiting for him in the garage with Michael's bike, and now? He'd gone and made Michael's grieving mother cry. She clutched Michael's sheets to her chest and turned around, sinking onto the bare mattress and sobbing so hard she couldn't hold herself up, and most of Peter wanted to go to her and comfort her, but there were those three goddamned words in his way.

But God said....

Peter turned around and walked out, wiping his face and pretending it wasn't wet. He saw the letters, one from Michael, one from Aileen, with Peter's name written on top in her handwriting, on the corner of his dresser, and couldn't face them—but he didn't want to leave them there, either, in case they should suddenly disappear.

He tucked them in his back pocket and found two sweatshirts he didn't give a shit about, then walked back down and made him and Bodi some sandwiches. He was starving.

He made sandwiches, grabbed the chips from the top of the fridge—he'd been the last person to go shopping, he could do this without remorse—and then some sodas from the fridge.

He hauled the whole works out into the thinning light and found Bodi pretty much where he'd expected to find him.

In the garage.

"You were gone a while," he said, coming out and wiping his hands on an old grease rag. Peter handed him a sandwich wrapped in a paper towel, and Bodi nodded thanks. "What's up?"

Peter swallowed through a tight throat. "Don't wanna talk about it."

Bodi rolled his eyes. "Shocker."

105

"Yeah?"

"Always were a tight-lipped little shit. Hey—is Michael's boom box out here still? All the CDs?"

"Yeah. Under the tool bench there."

Bodi waggled his eyebrows. "Wanna?"

Peter smiled back. "Yeah."

Hel*lo* Green Day! And Nickelback, Puddle of Mudd, Eminem, Sheryl Crow, Kid Rock, Offspring, and Coldplay—in short, everyone they'd listened to when Bodi and Michael had been in high school, including Springsteen, who had never been fashionable in their lifetime but whom Bodi had introduced to Michael, and Michael had adored as well. Michael had kept the CDs next to the boom box so they could listen to music while they worked. It was tradition. Peter ate his food while Bodi finished off his sandwich with one hand and went through the CDs with the other.

"Offspring—damn, we were out of date," he said with a full mouth. And then: "Oh, what the fuck? *Pink?* Whose CD was this?"

Peter swallowed in mortified silence. "Uhm, Michael got it for me for my birthday."

Bodi laughed. "God. What a mindfuck. You were never embarrassed about it, were you? Kids called you faggot, and you came home crying, and you got the shit kicked out of you, but never, not even once, did you say it wasn't true." Bodi shook his head, standing up with Green Day's *American Idiot* CD in his hand. "Michael and I started sneaking away, and I was so jealous of that, you know? Me and Michael, we were... were, like, only gay when we were alone together. You just looked at the world with those big eyes of yours, and you just *were*. It was awesome." Bodi looked at him levelly, and Peter deliberately threw his paper towel away. "It still is," Bodi said quietly, and Peter got closer, moving in until he was close enough to lick the little bit of mustard off Bodi's upper lip, which he did.

"I've loved you since I was twelve years old," Peter said, up front and conversational. "You had nothing to be jealous of. You have not once let me down."

106

Bodi looked down. "I will, Petey," he said softly.

Peter was so close he could see the faint green semicircle around Bodi's pupils, keeping his eyes from being true and complete blue, but only if you were close.

"I'll forgive you for that too, when it comes due," Peter promised, but Bodi didn't look reassured.

"Don't promise that one, okay?" But he said it softly and then gave in and leaned into the kiss Peter had been dying to give him.

His mouth was warm in the chilly evening, and Peter groaned a little, fell into his chest, and Bodi wrapped his arms around Peter's shoulders, careful not to touch him with greasy hands. Peter's hands were clean, and he had no reservations about slipping his hands into Bodi's back pockets and clenching his fingers tightly, kneading that tight, slight backside until Bodi went "nnnghhh" and thrust his groin closer to Peter's. He pulled back after a moment and gave Peter a mock glare.

"We've got work to do," he said, quirking his mouth in admonition.

Peter grinned. "I've got Michael's old sleeping bag," he said. "I can go back with you tonight, so, you know, you're not getting all worked up for nothing."

Bodi looked down. "Yeah?"

"Yeah."

"Then let's get something done!"

Peter laughed, and they got to work.

LATER that night Peter was lying on the sleeping bag, the stars scattered overhead so close they could have been watching from a black velvet theater. Peter hoped they were getting off while they watched, because Bodi was thrusting slowly in Peter's ass, with Peter's legs wrapped around his hips, and getting off was *definitely* on Peter's mind.

Bodi had tried to back out of sex when Peter had driven his car to the turnout, laden with bedding and pillows and Michael's old sleeping bag, and they'd set up under what Peter was coming to think of as "their tree." They'd stood for a moment, looking around, trying to understand the alien landscape of their favorite, most sacred place in dark.

"So," Peter said softly, "you'll have to go back to Arcata to get parts tomorrow?"

Bodi shrugged. "Yeah, may as well."

Peter thought that he really wanted to go with him, but.... "I should work on hammering out the forks and the frame," he said with a sigh. "If the funeral's on Saturday, we—"

"God," Bodi interrupted passionately. "Hell yes, we've got to get this done before that. I'm sorry—I know what I said, but I ain't fuckin' stayin' for that circus."

Peter nodded. "I... I think that might be the last thing I do in Daisy," he said apologetically.

"Good." Bodi nodded. "Good. Then... well. We'll finish the bike first."

And Peter heard what was in his voice. He wasn't planning to commit to what would happen after that. Peter understood—but he had plans too. They all involved Bodi.

"Look up there," Peter said instead. "The Milky Way is so bright." He smiled a little, finding comfort in the stars, in astronomy, like he had when he was a kid.

"You know their names," Bodi said. Their shoulders bumped, and Peter twined his fingers around Bodi's because he was tired of not touching.

"Yeah. I know their names and their luminosity and their absolute magnitude and their distance from earth and the number of planets in their systems...."

Bodi chuckled and put his hand over Peter's mouth. "Stop," he said, smiling. "You make me tired. You remind me of all the shit in

108

the world I don't know and you know already, and you ain't even been to school."

Peter licked the inside of Bodi's palm and Bodi shuddered and gasped, then jerked his palm away like that would take away the flood of sex that had heated the air between them.

"All you have to know," Peter whispered, swinging around so they were face to face, "is how to make love to me. You think we can do that again?"

Bodi nodded and flushed. "Maybe without that... you're still sore, Peter." He grimaced unhappily, and Peter kissed the corner of his mouth.

"I have lube in my pocket," he said softly, tracing the bottom of Bodi's lip and grinding his hips into Bodi's own. "It'll be better this time."

"Oh Jesus," Bodi breathed. "Where'd you get lube?"

"From my drawer when I grabbed my clothes." He'd gone back in the house long after he knew Aileen would be asleep to get his change of clothes for the morning and two pillows for the night to come.

"That doesn't mean—" Bodi muttered, and then Peter kissed him and figured he'd just persuade with his body if he couldn't reason with the man otherwise.

Bodi still tried to have sex without this one thing, this act that had been so brutal at the outset and had cost them both so very much, but Peter straight-out seduced him.

They kissed each other slowly, their skin heating, their kisses and touches becoming urgent moment by moment. It was cold, so when they finally separated, panting, they stripped off their clothes quickly, shoving them between the two sleeping bags so the clothes would help keep them warm and their body heat wouldn't let the clothes get too cold in the morning.

As soon as they were huddled under the sleeping bag, they kissed again, and Peter got to work. He broke off the kiss and moved down Bodi's chest, licking his nipples and letting them cool in the spring chill, nibbling on his stomach, his thighs, and then finally, his proud, unapologetic cock, which lengthened inside Peter's mouth. Peter played with his foreskin, pulled it back, trapped his tongue under there, moved the foreskin over Bodi's crown, and played with its looseness over and back…. So many fun things to do with that, he thought hazily, liking how Bodi's hardened flesh felt against his palate. Bodi's hands scrabbled at the sleeping bag and pounded the ground underneath it, and finally he grabbed at Peter's hair, which was long enough for him to get a good handful, and pulled back.

"Dammit!" he groaned. "Do you really want me to come in your mouth?"

"No, genius." Peter grinned, and he reached for his pants—which at this point were lying up by Bodi's head—and into the pocket. He pulled out the aforementioned little bottle of lubricant, which he'd bought the year before with some condoms when he'd driven to Crescent City. He hadn't told Bodi this, but the truth was he'd gotten them just in case, because when you waited until twenty-two to lose your virginity, you could never be too hopeful. He held the lubricant up in the moonlight and shook it so Bodi would know exactly what it was. "I told you, I came prepared!"

As he spoke, he turned the tube over and clicked the top, dumping lube on his fingers, before reaching his hand back to his naked bottom, tracing his crease and thrusting his fingers without preliminary into his hole. He was tender, yes, and sensitive—but also sensitized, and even the thrust of his fingers made him shudder. When he finished his thought, his voice was choked and breathless, and he let Bodi's cock bounce off his cheek and his tongue as he said, "I don't want you to come in my mouth, Bodi, I want you to come in my ass!"

Bodi started tugging at Peter's arms, and Peter went willingly, throwing one leg over Bodi's hips and holding his cock in place and… oh God… oh God… oh *yes!*

He slid onto Bodi's cock a little at a time, controlling the depth and the speed and holding his weight behind him on his hands as he bounced up and down and up and *ohholyfuckallujia!* Bodi's cool hand was gripping him and stroking, and his entire body was on fire and shivering as he watched Bodi's pale body beneath him in the soft-light darkness. He came, spurting across Bodi's chest, and he probably would have licked it off just for the sheer hungry eroticism of it, but Bodi wasn't done yet. Peter found himself hauled forward into Bodi's arms, and then Bodi rolled, their bodies still locked together.

Peter had only *thought* he'd orgasmed before, because now Bodi rose up, pushed, again and again and again, until he found Peter's sweet spot, the place that made him think about screaming, and then rode it unmercifully until Peter *was* screaming, inchoate things like "Oh God... fuck me, fuck me, fuck me, fuck me... please, please, please, oh *yes! Yes! Yes!* More, more, more, more, more, more, *fuck yes!*"—and hollering them loud enough to echo off the surrounding hills while Bodi ploughed into his body.

Bodi wasn't quiet either. "Gonna fuck ya, gonna fuck ya, c'mon, Petey, yell for me, yell real loud. *That's right, louder!*"— until Bodi's body seemed to shudder from pretty much his cock out, ending in his fingers, which shook in their grip on the inside of Peter's thighs, and Bodi cried, "Oh, Jesus, Peter, *love me!*" into the roar of the river and the whisper of the wind.

He collapsed against Peter, the two of them a sweaty, come-soaked mess, and Peter sacrificed his T-shirt to the cleanup. Finally they were less sticky, and wearing their boxers again, and tucked into the sleeping bags, and shivering, and Peter kissed Bodi's temple and whispered, "I do. You know that, right?"

Bodi sighed. "God, Peter—the shit you say during sex—"

"Counts," Peter said, his voice unequivocal in the darkness.

"Sure," Bodi breathed. "Yeah. You love me. Do you think... could you even imagine that I don't want to feel the same about you?"

"Do you?" Peter asked, not really afraid, because he was pretty sure he'd proven he was determined, but more curious. What did he have to do to prove himself some more?

"I don't want to make that sort of promise," Bodi said, shame in the way he couldn't look Peter in the eyes. "I'm a junkie—"

"Ex-junkie—"

"Like that makes it any better!"

"It's everything, Bodi. You didn't go back. Michael left you there, and it was a horrible place, and I'm so sorry you felt like you were there alone, but you left. You went to rehab and you came out and stayed clean. You didn't stay in that place. That's everything—don't you see? That you did what he couldn't? You got better!"

Bodi let out a sound that was part exasperation but mostly sorry. "But I haven't... how can I tell you words like that, Peter, when I haven't even told him good-bye!"

Peter relaxed against him. "You let me know when you can," he said softly. "You let me know when you've told my cousin good-bye. I'll be there. I've always been there."

Bodi banged his head back against the ground through the padding in apparent frustration. "Oh, God, Peter—you should have gone to college. I should have been... I don't know. A footnote or something."

Peter propped himself on an elbow and said, "Bodi, look at me."

Bodi did, his eyes colorless in the night.

"If you and Michael had lived, if you'd been happy, I would have gone on. I would have found someone. I would have been happy. But that's not what happened. And I'm not going to do that if no one's taking care of you."

Bodi scowled. "Six years, Peter—I've been doing it mostly right for six years—"

"And you shouldn't ever have to go it alone again. Isn't six years long enough? I mean, why not have anyone else in that time, if you weren't going to only do it with someone who really fucking matters?"

Bodi sighed then and wrapped his arm around Peter's shoulders and forced Peter's head back on Bodi's chest. "Yeah, God, you're fucking stubborn. You matter. You've always mattered. Don't rub it in, okay?"

The sleeping bag was an amazing place to sleep with a lover. It was intimate, and it trapped the smell of sex so that it lingered, permeating Peter's dreams along with the heat of Bodi's skin. When dawn began to break, the light unmercifully early, Peter tucked his head under the bag and was assailed by the smell of sex. He backed up into Bodi, who rolled over, half-asleep, and began to frot against him. Peter ground back and reached into his boxers, and in the warm dark they had a magic thing, a sleepy, half-conscious orgasm, that made it possible for them both to shudder and then ignore the dawn and fall back asleep.

The morning was a chilly exercise in getting dressed. First they had to run down to the river's edge to wet down a T-shirt so they could clean themselves up, and then they climbed back into the sleeping bag to warm up and pull on clean clothes. When they were done, they rolled up the sleeping bags together and hoisted them in the tree with the egg crate, then ate granola bars from Bodi's ice chest.

"You know," Bodi said thoughtfully as they took one last look around the spot to make sure it didn't look too lived-in, "I should probably go visit my sister's grave."

It was one of those weird moments when the world seemed to halt midspin and change axis to the point on which you were standing. Suddenly everything was dizzying around Peter, and he looked at Bodi to make sure he could stay on for the ride.

"Yeah," Peter said. "I should go too."

Bodi's face hardened like he was going to say Peter couldn't, but Peter forestalled him.

"I didn't go before," he apologized, and he winced at the hurt on Bodi's face. "I... I was mourning you and Michael," he explained, feeling weak. "It… I missed you both so bad, it took me a while to realize that I missed her too. I'm sorry."

Bodi nodded. "Tomorrow morning, then," he said quietly. "We can get some flowers." Then they both winced. Juliet had never been particularly fond of flowers. Bodi scowled. "Serves her right," he said sullenly. "If she'd fought to be happy half as hard as she fought everything else, she'd be making us miserable to this day."

Peter didn't have an answer to that. He grabbed Bodi's hand and kissed him and was relieved when Bodi's mouth opened under his. The kiss ended, and Peter kissed his cheek and said, "How about you leave the bike at Aileen's and take my car into Arcata. That'll make it easier?"

Bodi nodded and then grimaced. "It's logical, Pete, but it sort of sucks. I may hate the fuck out of Daisy," he said philosophically, "but you can't deny that it's a nice ride."

Peter sighed. It was true. The road wound enough to be challenging, but not enough to be truly dangerous, and the sheer beauty of the mountains and cleanness of the air were enough to take your heart out of your toes, if that's where it started out. "Well, if it's any consolation, you'll get to drive it again when you put Daisy in your rearview."

Bodi brightened. "Best thought I've had all morning—except for, you know, banging you again."

Peter grinned all the way back to the house.

BECAUSE THE NIGHT

BODI got back when Peter had about run out of things to do on the bike that didn't require all of the parts he was bringing, so that was serendipitous. He'd also gone to the Dairy Queen, where all the schoolkids working were too young to know who he was, and brought takeout. Peter was ravenous. Aileen had been taken to the church by friends, and he'd managed to sneak into the house to take a shower and get some more clothes, but the refrigerator was stuffed full of casseroles and what Peter was starting to think of as "funeral food" from the constant stream of visitors offering their condolences.

Peter thought about eating it, but… God. He couldn't. He just couldn't.

"Did you get some sandwich bread and PB&J in Arcata?" Peter asked a bit desperately, and Bodi nodded.

"Yeah. Granola bars don't cut it long-term, do they?"

Peter sighed. It felt like he had a chance to purge himself, fast from the "charity" offered by Daisy before he moved on to a new life with… well, with Bodi, right? He certainly wasn't planning to leave. Besides, he thought, looking around at the trees behind the house, giant redwoods that hadn't been cut down in most of the unused spaces of town, he really did love the mountains and the sea. He and his mom had lived in Sacramento before she'd brought him here, and he remembered looking outside the bus window with awe, thinking that he'd never known the world could be quite so beautiful.

He still thought this area of the world was beautiful. He just needed to get away from these particular people in it.

"Yeah." Peter sank his teeth into a triple cheeseburger with fried onion rings and barbecue sauce. "And if I eat like this every day, I'll get fat."

Bodi looked at him admiringly. "I'd wanna bang ya then too."

Peter found his face heating from Bodi's open appreciation. "Good to hear," he said, not able to meet Bodi's eyes. He found that he couldn't stop the slow grin. "I, uhm, you know. Backatcha."

Bodi's soft chuckle was low and sexy, and Peter needed to hear that sort of confidence enough to look up.

Bodi's eyes, those outer-space blue eyes that could be just suddenly focused elsewhere at a moment's notice, were very definitely, very certainly, fixed on Peter in his grease-stained jeans and T-shirt.

"So, uhm," Peter said, his voice rough and that damned smile not going away. "Uhm, tonight?"

Bodi's grin was unapologetic. "Uhm fuck yeah," he said, nodding, and Peter had to turn away to eat his cheeseburger, because otherwise he would have just stood there, leaning against his car and grinning like a fool, for most of the rest of the night.

After they had worked on Michael's bike for another three hours, they rode back to the water hole under the clean regard of the moon and stars. They got to the turnout and got off the bike and took off their helmets, and Bodi kissed him on the side of the road, where the gleaming light touched the edges of all the parts of the world that Peter loved best. Their breath came short and their hands wouldn't stop wandering so they scrambled down the drop-off and ran to the tree to set up their beds. When they were done, they unlaced their boots and stood up under the moon again and kissed all the parts of each other that they loved best, and the night ended on even more promise than it began with.

THE little cemetery was on the other side of the river from the church, and Juliet's headstone was a small, unadorned piece of polished granite amid the rest of the shaded graves.

Michael will be buried here.

The thought came out of nowhere, and Peter thought miserably that for that thought alone, it was a good thing that he and Bodi had come.

Uncomfortable at first, they looked up and down the uneven rows all planned around the occasional tree that was too vast and too ancient to cut down for mere humans, and when he realized that, for a moment, he was at peace. Michael would find a place here. Would it be over there? Or near that giant redwood in the back? There didn't seem to be anything there. Caskets had plain wood bottoms for a reason, Peter knew. How long would it take before Michael melted into the earth, became loam, had a chance to start anew, new molecules, new atoms, with maybe the pain and the bitterness leached away? Would there be a new Michael born somewhere, a Michael who might grow to adulthood and fulfill all his promises? That was a nice thought.

Then practical matters started settling in. Would Aileen pay for a nice headstone? Would the church? He thought that maybe the military would, and that it would have something about his service. The thought made him angry, because that service to his country felt like a betrayal to the people he'd left behind.

With an effort, Peter concentrated on the plain little headstone for Juliet Alison Kovacs and making sure his hand was on the small of Bodi's back, just sitting there, steady, in case Bodi needed it.

Bodi was making a list.

"Toldya to brush your teeth, take a bath, don't eat flowers, don't cuss at the teacher, toldya to say your prayers, thank God for your family, be respectful to the preacher, toldya to be nice to people, don't hurt things, stay away from sharp objects, do your schoolwork, toldya not to watch so much television, stay away from smooth-talking boys, don't give yourself up for free." Bodi closed his eyes, thought hard, apparently remembered more. "Toldya not to talk shit to my friends, not to give Mom a hard time, not to put your hand on the stove, brush your hair, clean your face, tell me or Mom when you needed girl stuff from the store, don't expect to have boobs at ten, don't expect to have boobs at sixteen even, don't sing too loud even when it's a really good song, don't piss people off to laugh at them...."

Peter moved his touch from the small of Bodi's back to clasp Bodi's hand, and Bodi squeezed him back so tight that Peter felt his tendons pop.

"Bodi?"

"Don't go swimming without us, don't watch television too late at night, stay off the Internet porn, you don't need to be looking at boy parts, too much makeup looks trashy, you were just fine without it, short skirts show your ass, big skirts make it look bigger, of course you're pretty don't even need to ask—"

"Bodi?" Peter whispered next to his ear, and Bodi stopped.

"Just had to make sure," he said back.

"'Bout what?"

"That I told her everything I needed to before she left."

Peter laid his head on Bodi's shoulder for comfort. "Yeah, Bodi. You did a real good job."

Bodi nodded, and his hand came up to the back of Peter's neck, firm and unyielding. For the moment, it was apparently really important to Bodi that Peter wasn't going anywhere.

THE night belonged to lovers—wasn't that how the song went?

They left the graveyard and went to the house to work some more on the motorcycle, and that night, they made slow, urgent love in their holy place until Peter felt like his body exploded with the stars.

And now, the next night, after another peaceful day spent working side by side, making that motorcycle as cherry and prime as it had never been when Michael had ridden it, Peter was watching Bodi lose it in the starlight again. Bodi's head was tilted back as he plunged into Peter, and his mouth was slack as every muscle in his body let go. Peter's come was already puddled on his abdomen and chest, and Bodi fell on top of him, panting, nuzzling his neck and laughing softly before sacrificing his own T-shirt this time to wiping them both off. Peter had been doing their laundry in the garage as they'd worked, and he and Bodi had continued to take showers in the bathroom at the house, waiting for Aileen to leave before slipping inside.

The letters he'd found on his dresser three days ago were now tucked into the back pocket of his most recent pair of jeans. He hadn't told Bodi about them either, and Aileen? She avoided them both like the fucking plague.

But still... the motorcycle was taking shape before their eyes, and the nights? The nights were... were this. Lovemaking. Perfection. No promises, no, but perfection just the same.

Peter didn't need Bodi's soft sound in the moonlight, though, to know that it couldn't last.

"What?" he asked, wiggling into his boxers again. Bodi stopped, up on his knees, and smoothed Peter's hair back from his face.

"Tomorrow, it'll be ready."

Peter nodded. "Yeah."

"We can do it tomorrow, then."

"Yeah. You take me down on the bike, I'll ride it up with you to the canyon."

Bodi touched his hair again before sliding into their little cocoon. "The funeral's the day after, right?"

"Yeah."

Bodi looked away. "I won't be there."

He'd said this before. Peter half expected it, but that didn't mean he had to agree. "Bodi—"

"Don't ask me to, okay? I don't have a damned thing to say to those people."

"How about 'fuck you'?"

Bodi grimaced and sat up under the sleeping bag, his chest pale in the moonlight. It was marginally warmer tonight than it had been, but his nipples were still puckered and his skin was still riddled with gooseflesh.

"Well, maybe that," Bodi was forced to concede, "but not at Michael's funeral. It's going to be a goddamned dog and pony show—everyone's going to be crying over the fucking flag and telling him what a good guy he is because he died for his country. He didn't die for his country, and he didn't die for their God—he died because they fucking killed him. I won't go." He didn't add *Nothing you can say will make me*, but he didn't have to.

Peter sighed and looked away. "Well then, I'll leave after the funeral and meet you in Ar—"

"Peter, don't make me do this."

Peter shook his head and got under the sleeping bag. "No," he said and opened his arm for Bodi to come snuggle.

"Just because you say that doesn't mean this conversation is over." Bodi stayed stubbornly upright, clasping his arms around his knees and shivering.

"Just because you say you and me are over tomorrow doesn't mean it's true." Peter propped his head on his hand and looked up at his lover—his true love—and tried not to just pop him one on the back of the head. "I'm going to school there, Bodi. I might as well live with you, because it would be *great* to do this in a bed, you think?"

Bodi sighed. "Michael wouldn't have wanted—"

Peter's temper flared. "Like you said, Bodi, Michael wasn't a saint, and his wishes in this matter don't count for shit. Now lay down and let me make you need me some more, it's fucking cold outside."

Bodi sighed and slid closer, and Peter kissed his cheek as Bodi pillowed his head on Peter's shoulder this time. "Peter, we're going to have to break up sometime."

Peter scowled. Bodi could say what he wanted, but it wasn't Peter who was being stubborn. "No we don't."

"Look, you didn't see the expression on your face when I told you I wasn't coming to the funeral. I've already let you down."

Peter's scowl stayed in place, just inches from Bodi's eyes. "And I've already forgiven you. Now shut up and kiss me, and let's get some sleep already. Tomorrow's gonna suck large."

Bodi's eyes were narrowed, so Peter kissed him instead, and the only reassuring thing about that was the way Bodi melted against him, melted in his arms, became a part of Peter's breathing without even trying.

Yeah, sure. Maybe Bodi would run away after tomorrow, and maybe Peter would have to pound down his front door to get back inside his sweet little shelter from the harsh and the cold. Not fun, no, but Peter had done it once, and he'd do it again, and Bodi wasn't ever going to be alone again.

That was his vow to Michael, and yeah, part of it was anger and part of it was affection, and Peter couldn't tell which part was which right now, but he would. Someday he would, and in the meantime, Peter would get the man Michael had tossed aside, and Peter would *never* let him be lonely again.

CANYON

"Aww," Nate was saying to Peter and Bodi as they gave the chrome one final polish. "You didn't have to go back to Arcata, Bodi. I would have fetched any part you wanted."

Nate had actually brought them their parts, as promised, the day after Peter had stopped at the auto parts store. They had still been at the swimming hole, so he'd left them on the porch with a note, and Peter was both surprised and pleased that he showed up the morning before the funeral.

Bodi looked at Nate soberly. "You know we're just doing this to kill it, right?"

Nate's eyes were a pretty green, but in shape they were much like Bodi's. Peter had wished wildly in high school that he could fall for those eyes, even though Nate was straight, because it would hurt less than loving Bodi when Michael got to have him. Right now, though, those eyes got really big. Nate opened and closed his mouth, then sighed and looked at Peter.

"You wouldn't want to keep it, would you, Peter? You know, as sort of your cousin's legacy?"

Peter and Bodi both caught their breath with shared pain.

"Whatever soul he had left is in his bike," Bodi said, wiping an imaginary speck of dust off the black-and-silver gas tank. "We need to set it free. We owe him that."

Nathan looked at the both of them with his arms limp at his sides. It was obvious that he'd tried. Peter had to admit to himself now that Nathan had tried. Peter had two years of high school left after Bodi and Michael had been outed and destroyed, and they'd been damned lonely ones. Peter remembered vividly that Nathan had sat next to him at lunch for three whole months the fall after Michael had left, and that Peter had probably not said more than six words to him. Michael hadn't been the only one who was angry. It was probably wrong to hold a grudge against every straight person in the world—especially when one of them had been your friend.

"I wish...," Nate said, and Peter looked at him, suddenly wanting to apologize for that frigid silence in their lonely corner of the tiny school quad.

"What?" he asked, as gently as he could.

"I wish folks knew," he muttered. "You were my friend, Peter. What this town did to your cousin... it made you not that way anymore. That's gotta be a bad thing."

Peter sighed. "I'm still your friend," he said, feeling foolish. "I was just really angry." He grimaced. "Still am. But not at you. Not now."

Nate smiled at him, and Peter returned it, but even he knew there were shadows under his eyes from the nights spent with Bodi on the sleeping bag at the watering hole, and from grief.

Nate's smile faded, and he looked wistfully at the bike. "It's beautiful," he said, thrusting his fingers through his thin hair. "You gonna do the thing right?"

Bodi looked at him speculatively. "Gasoline and an old T-shirt," he said, gauging Nate's reaction. He didn't mention that the T-shirt was Bodi's, one that Michael had given him in high school. Peter had noticed the day Bodi had shown up in it, but he was pretty sure no one else had.

Nate nodded. "The old canyon?" It was a few miles up above the swimming hole—you could see the plateau of it from the diving rock. The river actually missed the foot of the canyon by a good two hundred yards, and people had been wasting old cars off of it for years. You bought a lemon and fixing it was no longer an option? Put a brick on the gas pedal and drive that fucker down the side of the cliff, across the plateau, and off the old canyon. You wreck a car bad enough that the insurance people totaled it, but it still had one more go? Tow it to the canyon and let 'er rip. Environmentally sound? No. But it was cathartic—almost a party thing for people to do. They'd bring their friends and some beer and have a grand ol' send-off party for the fucking piece of crap that had let them down. So it wasn't PC, but it was tradition. And since tradition had destroyed Michael? Well, it seemed especially fitting.

"Yeah," Peter said. "Where else would we go?" He almost said, *Want to come with us?* but he didn't. This was going to be his and Bodi's moment—he couldn't make it bigger than that.

Nathan sighed. "Peter?"

"Yeah?"

"I'm on Facebook, on those rare moments when we get Internet. Do me a favor."

"What?"

"Wherever you end up, look me up, okay? I really would like to know."

Peter swallowed and clasped Nate's hand. They were both coming in with the shoulders to do the man-clasp thing, but Nate pulled him closer, their clasped hands between them, and said, "I missed you like hell, those last years in school."

Peter nodded and thought this grief might hurt more later, but now all he could think of was the gleaming, beautiful machine beside him and the fractured life it represented.

"I missed you too," he said, meaning it. "I'll look you up. I promise."

Nate pulled back and smiled through bright eyes. "You'd better. I'll hold you to that."

Peter shrugged, feeling foolish again. "I'm only going to be in Arcata. You could come visit, you know."

Nate's smile reached his eyes this time, and he got back in his little SUV and drove away.

"You don't want to go somewhere else?" Bodi asked. "Sacramento? Fresno? Chico?"

Peter, his chest pressed so tight from grief as it was, didn't have a graceful answer to that. "Shut up," he growled. "I'm not having this discussion again. Are we ready to go?"

"Yeah." Bodi stood, and the closed expression he'd worn when Nate had been there suddenly opened up some. "I'm glad you made your peace with him. He's a good guy."

"The best," Peter said, thinking wistfully of days spent helping Nate with his math and listening to his CD collection in his room. Nate might have been straight, but he'd always had a much more cosmopolitan taste in music than the average Daisy resident. His little room—white walled, square roof, matching sheets, comforters, and valances—had housed rap and pop and dance music, and Peter had loved it. When Peter thought back on it now, he figured Nate had probably been grateful to have a friend who didn't judge him on his taste in music in the same way he hadn't judged Peter for being unapologetically gay.

Peter vividly remembered the one real discussion they'd had about it and how wonderful it had been to just talk like it was a thing and not a crime.

"So, Peter?"

Peter had been sitting cross-legged on his bed, looking intently at the Pink CD case. "Yeah?"

"That gay thing?"

"Yeah?"

"What's it like?"

Peter shrugged. "You remember your first crush on a girl?"

"Kerry Dunstan." Nate had shrugged, then blushed. As far as Peter knew in the present, they'd been going out since senior year and never stopped, but they hadn't had their first date yet, not on that day, with the sharp winter sun cutting through the football pattern on Nate's window valance.

Peter nodded. "Yeah. I remember my first crush too."

"Bodi, right?"

Peter looked at him sharply, surprised. "How in the hell do you know that?"

Nate carefully studied the controls of his sound system and adjusted the EQ. "It's the way you look when you see him," he said softly. "If I didn't think gay was real already, just seeing how you look at him makes me think it's something we shouldn't pray away."

Peter had never told him how much that moment meant to him, and Nate never asked him about being gay again.

Peter remembered that moment, and he remembered something else. He'd never told Nate about Michael and Bodi, and he almost regretted it now. Nate, of all people, would have known what it had meant to him, but it hadn't been Peter's story to tell.

And now it was the entire town's legend to feed off of. When he thought of it that way, Peter *really* wished he'd told Nate back then—he felt like it would have been an offering for the things he didn't say later.

"We need to get out of here," he said, his heart so sodden with regret, the shit was dripping ice into his gut.

"I hear you, little brother," Bodi murmured, then stood up. "I've got the rag and the gasoline. You'll be right on my tail?"

Peter shook his head, his anger surging back. "It's a funeral, right?" he asked, and he smiled bitterly. "What's a funeral without a parade?"

Bodi sighed. "I'll be at the canyon when you're done showboating."

Peter leaned in and kissed the corner of his mouth until Bodi turned and there, in the driveway, in front of the entire town of Daisy, kissed him back. No one was there to see, but that didn't mean Peter didn't feel a little less angry as he pulled back and swung his leg over the bike, then fitted his helmet on and did the strap.

Michael had actually been teaching Peter how to ride a motorcycle before he'd wrecked his bike. Peter had been about to go get his license when that had happened, and, well, besides Michael rethinking that whole "let's put my beloved younger cousin on a motorcycle" thing, other shit had also come up. Peter hadn't regretted selling his first motorcycle even a little bit.

So Peter had forgotten why he'd loved it, forgotten why Michael and Bodi had loved it. He'd *thought* he'd remembered this last week, coming and going on the back of Bodi's bike, but he'd forgotten what it was like to actually *control* the beast.

He had to contain a visceral shudder on the back of the bike, because oh *God*, was that power outrageous. The engine roared and the wind whooshed, and all that sound drowned out everything but the ferocity of the bike, how smooth she took the curves, how good the air felt on your face, and the unique, clear threads in the tangle that was your heart.

And Michael's machine? Oh, she was a beauty. They'd pounded out most of the dents, straightened the forks, and Bodi had cleaned and reassembled the engine—this bike didn't purr, she *roared*, like a pissed-off lion, one who had been languishing too long in the zoo. Peter had ridden the thing back and forth along the little block that made up the road behind Daisy's main drag, pissing off the neighbors, the day before. Today, he was riding her right down his hometown street, and the glorious, fuck-you noise of her!

Peter used to hate the sound of this bike in particular and motorcycles in general. He would be reading in his room, and Michael and Bodi would just keep starting their project du jour up and stopping it and starting it up and stopping it, all to see if their hard work was paying off. He'd come out all pissed off but trying to be polite about it and practically *weeping* for them to stop so he could concentrate. Finally, when he was almost fifteen, Michael laughed and ruffled his hair and then gave him a helmet—this exact helmet, the brown one with the blue racing stripes—and put him on the back and took him through town. Driving the bike now, Peter could remember that moment, holding onto his handsome cousin's waist and thinking that the world owed Michael this kind of grandeur, because that was just how wonderful Michael was.

So that's what he was thinking as he ripped a hole through Daisy with that spectacular primal metal scream. He opened the bike up, revved her at all the stops, made her howl for the good people of Daisy. He rode from one end to the other of the half-mile main drag, with its faux vintage façades and its charming, tourist-friendly banners out front. More than one disapproving face pressed against a dusty window, and more than one man in a plaid shirt and khakis or woman in a denim skirt came out and stood in the entryway of a business or the porch of a house as he made his second and then third circle of Daisy. Warren came out on his third pass for a moment with excitement on his face and then a sort of burning fury as Peter flipped him the bird and just kept on riding, leaving the echoes of that brilliant engine in his wake.

The trip up to the canyon was magical. He'd snuck into Michael's room the last time Aileen had left the house and stolen the brown leather jacket he'd used to wear riding. It was cracked and needed oiling and repair, but the wind in the shade didn't bother him, and the play of light and dark, of black road, green trees, and sunlight on the hillsides was dazzling and lovely. Daisy might have been a black mold spot on the skin of the earth, but the apple that surrounded it was sweet, and Peter still loved it. It was a good thing to remember on a day like this.

The canyon was up above the swimming hole by only a few miles. In fact, you could see the bluff when you were standing on the diving rock; it was like the rock's deadlier, more implacable cousin. Bodi had parked his bike at the turnout, but if they were going to do this thing—this spectacular, painful, gorgeous good-bye—Peter was going to have to ride it over the curb and down a few feet of scrub to the plateau above the bluff. It was a scary wrestling match with the handlebars and the revving engine, and for a moment, Peter was afraid he wasn't going to be able to stop the chrome and metal monster, and that he'd just go skidding off the edge of the bluff with the bike, a fitting send-off for his cousin, probably. But not the one he wanted, ultimately.

He burned his calf on the exhaust manifold through his jeans like a rookie and almost dumped all that polished chrome, but he eventually came to a halt at the base of the first drop with about twenty feet of flat mesa between him and the edge.

Bodi had been waiting for him at the bottom of the first, mild drop, and the expression on his face as Peter stood, panting, the big metal dragon finally tamed and rumbling at his side, was drawn back at the mouth and scrunched at the forehead.

"Jesus... oh fucking Jesus—Peter, you stupid bastard, you should have parked up there and asked for my help. Oh holy fucking God... I almost shit my pants."

Peter smiled, triumphant through the sweat. "I got it, Bodi. No worries. It's okay."

Bodi shook his head, his white-knuckled hands clenching his helmet strap. "No, man. You don't get it. It's not fucking funny, and it's not fucking no worries. Those six years, I was living my fucking life, and I kept thinking about you sleeping next to Michael's room, and... God. It just gave me peace. You get that? Thinking about you, asleep—it gave me peace. I see you go off the edge of this fucking cliff with that bike, and that's no peace, and I'd probably take my bike off the edge with you. *Fuck,* Peter, you can't take risks like that."

Peter let the smile go and took Bodi seriously. "Okay, Bodi," he said quietly. "I hear you."

Bodi nodded and swallowed. "Turn off the bike," he said after a moment where the shaking of his hands on his helmet let Peter know he was struggling with himself. Peter did and followed Bodi back to the slope, where there was a little shade and a rock to sit on. They sat down and looked out over the canyon to the next tree-covered mountainside, and Peter's heart cramped in his chest. It was a long, long stretch to the other side of the canyon. It had always seemed like the other side of the world. If he stared, and imagined, and hoped enough, maybe he could see Michael over there, under one of the bigger trees, reading a book, listening to music, planning a future.

"He had all these plans," Peter said into the silence. "Do you remember those notebooks? All these pinstriping jobs, all these bike designs—his mind was constantly in motion, and it all...." Peter's voice dropped, and for the first time since he'd knocked on Bodi's door, the enormity of what he'd done in the last five days hit him. He'd stolen Bodi from Michael. Yeah, Michael was gone—but.... Peter took a deep breath, then another, and forced himself to finish that sentence.

"It all revolved around you," he said, but the saying of it caught in his throat, and Bodi looked at him with darkened eyes.

"You think it didn't revolve around you too?" Bodi let out a little puff of bitterness. "Man, the last thing he said to me in rehab was 'Don't tell Peter. God, Bodi—I want him to remember me like I was someone.'"

Peter swallowed. "He was someone, Bodi. He was our fucking world." Peter put his hand in his back pocket. "He sent me his letter. He sent me a couple of postcards while he was gone—mostly 'I'm alive, I miss you'. A postcard from France, one from Germany, Turkey, Israel. But he never said anything. Nothing real. But...." Peter's throat was so tight, his chest hurt and his ears hurt and breathing hurt. "He sent me his letter. Haven't read it yet."

Bodi nodded. "I expected to get one," he said. "Got the same postcards, probably, but for four years, I expected to get one."

"Not the last two?"

Bodi shook his head and looked out over the canyon. No. He'd obviously not been expecting anything from Michael in the last two years.

"I didn't know it," he said. "Until rehab... God. Not even a kiss on the cheek or a touch on the hand. He just stayed in the doorway the entire time, telling me he was leaving, and then he left. I didn't know it until right then, but... that boy... my boy... he died when my sister did, pretty much." Bodi's gaze across the canyon never wavered. "It's like... like he was walking around, talking to other people, shooting a gun at other people, which just blows my mind, and the whole time, the person we knew? He was so long gone. It's like his ghost came back into my life to teach me to shoot up—which works, right? Ghosts are supposed to be evil and twisted and not the real person at all? Michael never would have done that. Our Michael. Our Michael wouldn't have left me in rehab. That was ghost Michael, and he was just here so I didn't lose everyone at the same time."

Peter couldn't look across the canyon anymore. He could only look at Bodi. His bleached brown hair was loose around his shoulders, and his eyes were so dark with pain they had almost lost their blue. His lean face was clenched like a fist against what was fighting to come out, and he was picking at his grease-stained fingernails. While Peter watched, he ripped one off past the cuticle until it bled.

Peter reached over and covered Bodi's hands with his own.

"We're here to say good-bye to him," he said quietly, and Bodi nodded.

"And to each other."

"No."

Bodi stood up. "You deserve—"

"Shut that noise the fuck up. That's not why you want to do this." Peter stood up and stared at Bodi. It hurt his eyes, but Bodi, even broken, even wrong, fed his soul.

"Don't tell me what I'm thinking!" Bodi snapped. "I'm not stupid, Peter! I know what I want!"

"Yeah?" Peter snarled back. "Do you really want to do this now? Do you *really* want to stop seeing me? Be honest, Bodi—and don't feed me that 'it's for your own good' bullshit, because I ain't buying!"

"'Ain't'," Bodi mocked. "Did you just hear yourself say 'ain't'? I heard it."

Peter blinked. "So what."

"So—what was the last book you read, Peter?"

"*Social Engineering Through Literature*," Peter said blankly. "Why?"

"Auuuughhhh!" Bodi dug the heels of his hands into his eyes and screamed, doing a squat-stand in pure frustration. "*What are you doing with me?* Michael left because he felt like all of his insides—all of the things that made him sweet and brave and trust people—that all died. What do you think staying with me is going to do with you? Even if you go to school? You'll die—all that bigness in your heart, it'll get as small as this town, or Arcata, which is like a gnat's spit bigger. And you'll hate me." Bodi pulled in a breath and let it out through a sputter of tears. "And you'll leave. Do you really think I can watch that happen again?"

Peter closed his eyes. "Don't you have enough faith to try?"

"Faith?" Bodi's voice was a raw cackle. "Faith? It took all the faith I had to come back to this three-spit town. Faith? We're offering Michael's soul to pagan fucking gods, Peter, do you know why?"

Peter swallowed. "Because the church is fucked—"

"And we've lost our faith." Bodi nodded bitterly and shook his head.

"Well, you won't lose your faith in me," Peter determined, but he was shaken, shaken to the pith and core, by the idea that he might not be enough to convince Bodi to love again. He looked at the bike, gleaming so bright he had to turn his eyes away, and growled, honest to Christ *growled*, stalking over to the damned thing while ripping off the leather jacket. He hung the jacket over the handlebars, making sure it was secured before twisting off the gas cap.

"Start it up?" he asked, and Bodi nodded.

"Don't we want to say something first?" he said, and Peter grimaced. It was a funeral, after all.

"Yeah," he said, his anger and his grief suddenly battling his throat for full control. He made a raw sound as he turned the key and started the bike up, that beautiful, furious roar almost convincing him to call this off and wrestle the damned thing up the hill. Then Bodi came up with his T-shirt—that faded, beloved black Green Day T-shirt, with the red hand clenched over the white grenade—and wadded it up and shoved it into the gas tank.

Something had to explode, that was for sure. Bodi stood across from him, both of them with their hands on the brakes, Peter ready to kick the thing into gear when Bodi pushed up the kickstand.

"I loved him," Peter shouted over the roar of the engine. "I fucking loved him. But he left you alone, and he broke you. You were everything I ever wanted, Bodi Kovacs, and he fucking broke you. I want this thing gone, I want it away from us, so you will let me fix you again!"

Bodi shook his head and swallowed. They were both crying and shouting, because that noise was drowning out all subtlety and all they had left was the ripped and bleeding grief. "I want you to be happy!" he shouted. "If I thought for a minute that I could make you happy—but I wasn't enough to keep him, and I'm not good enough to keep you, and I won't fuck you up like he did to me! It's the only thing left to give him!"

"Fuck him!" Peter screamed so loudly his throat was sore. "*Fuck him!* Light this fucker up, Bodi, and destroy it, and then we can have each other!"

Bodi screamed, another primal stomach scream, and dumped gasoline over the tank and the engine, and then said, "Put it in gear!"

Peter did, and Bodi pulled out a tiny butane lighter and kicked the kickstand back, and as he and Peter balanced the bike, the gear caught and the momentum took over, and he lit the gas-soaked T-shirt on fire.

They both jumped back as a lovely *fwoosh!* engulfed the bike, and it went hurtling across the top of the bluff and off the edge into the rocky canyon below. They followed, screaming and hollering, then skidded to a halt a few feet from the edge and watched as it arced in a fiery crest down into the metal skeletons of other people's immolated dreams. It crashed, and they watched, half hoping for an explosion, but none happened. It just burned, bilious black smoke rising thickly to heaven, taking with it whatever part of Michael had been trapped inside this thing he'd once loved.

They stood, side by side, chests heaving, making sure that none of the underbrush caught, or the drying grasses on their mesa, and Peter was aware that he was sobbing, and Bodi was sobbing next to him. He grabbed Bodi's hand and jerked him back to their place in the shade, with the rocks to sit on, and sat down, hauling Bodi into his arms so they could howl out their anguish together.

Nothing was resolved, nothing was fixed, but Michael was gone, and they mourned him, screamed grief into each other's chests, beat on each other's backs with closed, impotent fists, because it was all they had left to do.

VOICES

BODI broke out of his arms before the tears had entirely stopped. He took one last look around the canyon, probably to make sure they hadn't set anything on fire. Peter did the same: the bike was reduced to a blackened frame, but there were no more flames to spare. Bodi started working his way up the hill, as grim as Peter had ever seen him. Peter put on his helmet so he could use his hands to climb, and followed, and they were both sweating and dirty and irritable by the time they got to the top.

Bodi swung onto the motorcycle and revved it up, waiting while Peter swung up behind him. His car was back at the swimming hole, and Bodi had to at least take him that far before he said his final piece. Peter wasn't ready to give up the war yet, but he was tired and heartsore. He badly needed to regroup and sort out his head before he launched another sortie into Bodi's damaged territory.

If nothing else, he needed to wash the stink of Michael's funeral pyre off his skin.

The ride home reeked of it, making even Peter's strong hold around Bodi's stringy waist a bitter thing. Bodi's skin was warm and a little moist under his shirt and his leathers, and Peter was torn savagely between needing to touch, needing to have, and needing to rage. His blood was boiling so hard it was like he could feel the bubbles of fury moving under his skin.

Bodi pulled up to the turnout to park, and Peter dropped his helmet as his feet hit the ground. He went scrabbling down the bank so fast that he tripped and threw himself backward, slid down the hill on his ass and skinned his elbows on the hard-scrabble dirt without slowing. He took off toward Bodi's campsite, ripped off his

135

shirt, and stopped to kick off his shoes and socks, leaving them as he ran for the rock. He left on his boxers—mostly because he was in too much of a hurry—and climbed up the side of the rock. When he got there, he hurtled blindly over the edge, leaping into the water and screaming as the cold of it closed over his head and shocked his scrapes. He flailed, coming up sputtering and with every intent of allowing the current to bear him past the landing rock. He didn't care if he was pulled under, he didn't care if he was dashed against the rocks in the rapids that roared through town—he wanted to be purged of the smell of mourning, and he wanted to be gone.

He didn't hear Bodi's second splash, but he did feel that surprisingly stringy, tough arm coming up under his armpit and across his chest as Bodi dragged him forcibly to the landing rock. He didn't struggle, not after he realized who had him, and when their feet touched the rock—which was covered in about four feet of water before it dropped off—they both crouched down and then slogged their way up to shore.

Peter was shivering, because *Christ*, that water was all snowmelt, and his scrapes and his still tender nose and the burn on his calf were all shocked and aching with cold.

And Bodi was furious.

"What the hell did you think you were doing?" Bodi yelled, grabbing him by the shoulder and whirling him around as their feet touched the warm, flat granite of the dry part of the rock.

"I was dirty." Peter's voice was a low gravel, howling angry and striving hard to be rational, striving hard not to crack, not to snarl or snap or howl.

"So you're just going to what? Let the river carry you? Wash up behind the fucking insurance guy's house?" Arthur Caufield—the guy got dead animals washing in through his little inlet/beaver dam all the time. When they were kids, he used to pay them money to fish out the carcasses and bury them on his property so they wouldn't stink. He was a pillar of the church, one of the loudest voices in denouncing Michael and Bodi and the supposed sin they'd been committing the day Juliet had died. The thought of washing up in his backyard, bloated and horrifying, gave Peter a whole lot of macabre satisfaction.

"Yeah," Peter said, and his smile must have been damned near deranged. "Yeah. That's exactly what I want to do. I want them to feel it, Bodi. I want them to feel it like we do. It wasn't fair—"

"They didn't kill him, Peter," Bodi said with an exaggerated patience, and suddenly Peter *hated* him with a red fierceness that limned his vision.

"The *hell* they didn't! They killed him! They killed whatever was inside of him that was decent, that loved you, and then he went and killed whatever was inside of *you* that could have loved me!"

"*He* killed it!" Bodi snarled, his own rage seeming to besiege him just like Peter's. They were face to face, chest to chest, their breath exploding against the other's face in pants. Peter could feel the heat thrown off Bodi's skin as he grasped Peter's shoulders and shook him, and Peter let him, backing up, guiding him, to their lover's tree, where he had some half-formed notion of fucking this rage into the loam at their feet.

"He did *not!*" Peter shouted back, shaking from the idea. "It wasn't his—"

"I was still me, Peter—*I* was still here! He could have come and lived with me—he could have! But he didn't! He wanted to fucking prove something to this town more than he wanted to come and make a life—"

"They drove him to it—"

"*Well he could have gone another way!*" Bodi snarled, the mildness, the kindness that Peter had remembered completely gone, a black rage pouring from his eyes like the red one was ripping through Peter's. Peter remembered, not four days ago, in this very spot, begging Bodi to be mad at Michael, and now Bodi *was* mad at Michael, and Peter was trying, *God* he was trying to be mad at anyone else *but* Michael.

He found himself holding Bodi's cheeks and nodding. "You're right," he said, his voice dropping to a whisper. "You're right. But you're threatening to leave me, too, and I'm pissed, because you're still alive, but you won't fight for me, Bodi. Why won't you fight for me?"

Bodi closed his eyes. "I told you... Peter... I told you... I'm not the man you're going to need—"

"*Shut up!*" Peter yelled and then silenced him with a kiss.

It could have been a hard kiss, a punishing kind, like their first kiss in this place, but it wasn't. It was savage and desperate, yes, but also yearning... tender. Bodi groaned and cupped the back of Peter's neck and moved his tongue slowly, surely, needing and taking, and Peter responded, giving Bodi everything that the baptism of grief had left him. Suddenly their chests were pressing together, and they were skin on skin, and Bodi's smooth skin, his tiny bit of chest hair, it felt oh so good against Peter's own.

Peter took his surrender and dominated, pushing him back against the tree until Bodi grunted with the impact, and then kissing him harder, until everything about Bodi was boneless, yielding and needing. Peter pulled back, still so close his lips brushed the skin of Bodi's chin, his neck, his ear, as Peter spoke.

"Just like this, Bodi," he whispered. "You and me, we feel just like this. And it's just us here, no one else. You really going to walk away from that?"

Bodi tipped his head back against the tree and closed his eyes. Peter kissed his neck, his collarbone, down to a pink nipple, which he sucked in hard and fast. Bodi's hands knotted in his hair. "Unnnhh... God," he breathed. "Peter... Peter, I want...."

Peter dropped to a squat, kissing Bodi's stomach while he pulled down his sodden underwear, and took Bodi's river-cold, hardening cock into his warm mouth. Bodi's hands tightened, and he pressed Peter's head convulsively, pulling him closer until his cock was all the way in Peter's mouth and brushing the back of his throat. Peter had gotten good at this in the last week, and he knew when to pull back, knew how to use his tongue to swirl around the head, and knew about sucking hard and swallowing, so his lips were brushing Bodi's curling hair. Bodi's groan ripped the forest quiet to shreds.

"Peter," he groaned, and then he started moving, one of his hands disappearing from Peter's hair. Bodi shifted again, one shoulder coming away from the tree, and Peter went to grab his hip to push him back, and then Bodi did something Peter never thought to hear him do. "Peter, please... please...," he begged. Peter kept tasting him, kept swallowing him down, and Bodi was doing something, spreading his legs, fumbling behind him. Peter reached between his spread thighs and tugged on his balls, appreciating the hissed breath and almost desperate grunt of pleasure Bodi made when he did that, and then Peter felt back further.

Bodi had two fingers lodged in his own asshole, slickened with spit, and Peter's cock gave a giant aching throb.

He pulled back and teased Bodi's crown with his tongue. "You want me inside you," he stated, his skin cold with anticipation. He'd watched them making love, watched them moving together. Not once had he ever seen Bodi bottom. As far as he knew, it had never....

Peter shuddered, pulled Bodi into his mouth again, and tried not to come from the taste of him, from Bodi's hands in his hair, from the thought of doing this thing, this one thing, that Bodi had never done, of having this one part of Bodi that Michael never had.

"Please, Peter," Bodi murmured, and Peter stood slowly, making sure their skin stroked together the entire way up.

"Why?" he asked, searching Bodi's puzzled blue eyes and aching for the answer.

Bodi looked away, past Peter's shoulder, to the place where the sky watched over the river, and sighed, his body melting into Peter's like he was ceding his control away, ceding any pretense he had to being in charge.

"'Cause...," Bodi muttered. He moved his fingers inside his body and threw his head back and howled. Peter sucked on his neck, moved down to his collarbone, down to his nipple, while he continued to stroke Bodi's cock, tugging the foreskin up over the head and back down again, hearing the small gasps and whimpers that came from Bodi's throat as he did.

Peter released his nipple, gave it a sweet, tart bite, and whispered, "Because why?" against his skin.

Bodi kept that tight clench in the hair at the nape of Peter's neck, and he tilted Peter's head up so Peter's gaze could meet his own.

"Because I never gave it, that's why." Slowly, painfully, he pulled Peter up to his level. "You get something no one else gets. It's all I got to give."

Peter claimed his mouth again, almost angrily, because it was not true, it was *so* not true, but he wanted it, oh *God* did he want something, some part of Bodi that his cousin never claimed.

"You ready yet?" he asked, pulling away. He put his cupped hand under his mouth and spat on his palm a couple of times, and when he was done, Bodi—one hand still behind his back—let go of Peter's hair with the other long enough to hold Peter's hand in his own and spit into the center as well. It was like schoolboys getting ready to promise something, only... only....

Bodi's eyes closed and his back arched, and his cock bobbed urgently against Peter's thigh. Peter shoved his wet hand down the front of his boxers and stroked, lubricating the end as much as he could.

"This might not be comfortable," he breathed, squeezing his cock as much as oiling it.

"You'd know." Bodi's arm jerked, and he shuddered as he stretched himself. Peter put two hands, gentle ones, on his shoulders, and turned him around until he was facing the tree. Bodi bent over, and for a moment Peter had a view of that stringy, sinewy body bared just for him. Bodi's fingers were buried in his backside, moving in and out, scissoring wide and then closing and thrusting in.

"I don't want to hurt you," Peter whispered behind him, and Bodi tilted his head so Peter could kiss the corner of his mouth.

Peter did, then glided his lips back over Bodi's cheek, into the cup of his ear.

"Can't help it."

Peter grasped Bodi's wrist and tugged until Bodi pulled his fingers out of his own body and grasped Peter's cock behind him. Bodi's palm was cool and his fingers were warm as he wrapped his hand around Peter's erection and backed slowly onto it.

Peter gasped. The heat and clench of Bodi's rectum around Peter's cock... oh... oh.... Bodi backed up a little more, engulfing him, the spit and precome making Peter's cock just slick enough, just wet enough for Bodi to keep moving, for that heat to grasp him completely. Bodi's breath was labored, grating harshly in his throat, and when Peter was completely embedded, he buried his sweating face against his arm and let loose with a low moan. Peter kissed his back and his neck through the sweat-soaking hair while he fought the imperative for his hips to move.

"Peter... you've got to...."

"Are you okay?"

"Not like this...." Bodi panted. "Not until it's finished."

Peter pulled back and thrust forward, his whole body shivering with the rightness of it, and Bodi moaned into his arm.

"Better?"

"God, yeah. Do it again."

Peter pulled back and thrust forward again, letting Bodi's groan echo in the seat of his balls, and again, and again. Bodi's noises became less pained, less forced, and began to relax into pleasure sounds, while the clench of his body around Peter's grew so tight, so excruciatingly perfect, that Peter thought all he'd have to do to come was just bury himself and let Bodi spasm around him. He didn't, though. Bodi had begged him to move, so move he did, and Bodi's next sound was soft and needy. Peter whispered, "Stroke yourself, Bodi... come on, sweetheart, let it be good."

Bodi's next sound was even needier, and one of the hands against the tree dropped. The muscles in his back played as he stroked himself and his clench around Peter's cock intensified, grew tighter, until Peter could hardly move. Peter put his hands on Bodi's hips and pushed forward so he could pull back and thrust again, and Bodi's needy sound turned to a growl as Peter slammed into him. Again... oh God, again... and... and.... *"Fuck!"* Peter snarled, and Bodi groaned again and shuddered and shuddered while Peter wrapped both arms around his shoulders and convulsed inside his body, coming and coming and coming.

THAT night Peter sat in his bedroom and looked around.

It was a rectangular room, and small. The first room at the top of the stairs was Michael's, and it was bigger, with the bigger window, but Peter had always sort of liked his little room. It had a small window that looked back into the woods because nobody lived behind them, and the twin mattress might be a little short now, but then, Peter had never sprawled. He'd always curled, tried very hard to make sure the world didn't see him. He was there on his aunt's sufferance. If the world saw him, they might send him away, and since his mother had needed to leave, he didn't have anyplace left.

The bedspread was old. It had been bought at a hand-me-down store when Peter was seventeen and working his own job. It was simple, plain dark blue, but unlike the one with the cartoon characters on it, it had been Peter's and not Michael's hand-me-down. The sheets now, the clothes, the books stacked up on cinderblocks—they were all his. The computer too. Peter sat on that bed with the plain metal frame and wondered how much of this stuff he could put in his car. He reckoned all of it.

That beautiful, sun-dappled, water-rushing elemental moment of holding Bodi in his arms and feeling like the world was his could not have lasted. It was spring in the mountains and not warm enough for them to stay there naked, for one thing, but not the only thing.

Peter had felt Bodi's painful attempts to disengage their hearts while he was still entrenched in Bodi's body.

Bodi moved forward until Peter fell out, but by then, Peter had cupped his shoulders and turned him around.

"We'd better dress," Bodi said weakly, looking toward the clothes lying scattered on the ground.

Peter stopped him then, took his mouth, relieved when he surrendered immediately. When they weren't kissing, weren't touching, apparently he could try to detach himself from Peter's love, but when Peter was parting his lips, sweeping his tongue inside, palming his bare skin? Bodi was his. It was a start, a thing to hope for, and Peter would cling to that hope until his fingers ached.

Bodi fell away from him when the kiss was done, propping up his naked body on the tree that had sheltered him and Michael and now him and Peter, but which would offer no comfort at all.

"Peter—"

"You'll leave today. I get it. But I'll come find you."

"You'll learn to hate me."

"You'll learn to love me first."

"Don't you see? There is nothing left in me to fight for you. Don't you deserve to be fought for?"

"Don't you?"

Bodi closed his eyes. "I tried. Man, with Michael, I tried. Can't you just... just take this thing with us and call it good? Can't you give me one good thing to remember?"

Peter's chest ached, the brilliant flare of orgasm fading from his body like a painting in the sun. He leaned forward and rested his forehead against Bodi's.

"Bodi?"

"Yeah?"

"There's only one thing I'm going to ask of you right now, okay?"

143

Bodi's hands came up, palming the smooth skin of Peter's biceps as he absently ran his thumbs tenderly up and down near the join of Peter's arms. "What do you want?" he asked, seemingly fascinated by his touch on Peter's skin.

"Don't give up."

Bodi kept his attention focused on his thumb, which was moving gently, and Peter let him for a moment.

"Bodi?"

"Okay," Bodi murmured. "Okay. You're going to need all the hope you can fathom for tomorrow. I won't rip it away now."

But he didn't meet Peter's eyes. They got their clothes and dressed, shivering in the shade. Peter didn't wash, and he didn't suggest Bodi go do it either. He wanted Bodi on his skin for as long as possible. They sat down side by side to lace up their boots, and Peter watched Bodi wince and felt bad.

"Man, you've got to ride all the way back—"

Bodi pulled himself from whatever reverie had been calling. "It'll be okay, really. I'll get on the back of the bike and…." For a moment he looked dreamy and young, and Peter felt a chill.

"And what?"

Bodi shook his head. "I'm at peace on the bike, Peter. I won't even feel it."

That chill got worse.

"Bodi?"

"Yeah?"

"Promise me you'll make it home."

Bodi startled a little, and understanding seemed to pass over him. He frowned for a moment as though asking himself a hard question, and then he squinted at Peter, probably because the sun was at Peter's back, and shook his head.

"I promise I won't fuck up this day for you any more. Man, the least I could do is let you hate me all on my own and not for mucking up Michael's funeral, right?"

A sudden shaft of sorrow. "Yeah. Bodi?"

"Yeah?"

"That hating thing isn't going to happen. Just drive home safe, okay?"

"For you, Peter? Absolutely."

They stood up then, and Peter checked his front pocket for his keys and his back pocket for his letters. They were both there, the crackle of the paper subdued but still intact. Yeah. Too many bad things going on today and tomorrow to have to worry about Bodi.

Peter helped Bodi lash his little cooler and his duffel bag and bedroll to the bar behind the bitch seat, and then Bodi leaned on the bike for a moment, and Peter took his cue to move into Bodi's space.

"I'll come for you," he said quietly, looking at those eyes, hoping to see them actually focused on his face.

They were. "Don't," Bodi said, so simply that Peter's heart failed a little.

"I will."

Bodi sighed. "Let me imagine you happy instead."

A shaking anger clenched Peter by the throat, and he grabbed the back of Bodi's head and pushed him in for a savage kiss. Bodi returned it gently, and Peter's anger dissipated, leaving only a misty sort of despair.

"You could make me happy," Peter said, kneading Bodi's shoulders while they both controlled their breathing. "You could. If you'd only let yourself."

Bodi closed his eyes. "God, Peter. Brave feels so far away."

"You go find your brave. I'll come find you."

They parted then, but Bodi's eyes never really met his. Bodi put his helmet on and started the bike. He ripped out of the turnout, away from the one place where he'd ever really been loved, without a backward look.

Peter stood there for a moment in the swirl of dust left by the bike and got into his little red car, thinking he felt as empty as the sky.

SITTING in his tiny room—the one home he'd known as a child and adult—thinking about that moment, he felt no less empty. Bodi, whom he'd wanted all his life, might still be out of reach, and after those few stolen nights, the thought was insupportable. Peter's one sliver of hope, from the moment Michael had left, was that if Michael didn't want Bodi, maybe, just maybe....

Michael. Goddamn him. Fucking damn him to—

Except according to the town, he really was in hell, wasn't he?

Peter suddenly longed for his cousin with so much force his stomach cramped, and he had to, had no choice about it, pulling out the two battered letters in his pocket.

The first thing he realized as he started scanning Michael's letter was that Michael had written it not two days before he was killed. In fact, it wasn't the letter Peter had thought it was at all.

Dear Peter—

Don't worry, this isn't my final letter. Mom will get that one, if it comes. The thing is, I just finished a sex party in the supply closet. I know, TMI, right? But DADT is over, and it's the only time I get touched these days, even if it's not gentleness. I find that's what I miss most about Bodi. He'd just put his hand between my shoulders and rub, and it doesn't matter how much I'm with anyone else, when I'm done, that place hurts, like blue balls only worse. So there I am, that place on my back aching, and I'm crawling back into my bed, feeling used and tired and empty, and it suddenly hits me harder than most days, that you must be really disappointed in me.

You used to look up to me so much. You send me letters once a month, and I'm so ashamed, I can't even reply. I tell you I'm alive. I think of you sleeping in your bed, and I know it's stupid, but I think of you young. You're grown up by now—you think I haven't read your letters, but I have. But I think of you, twelve, and you used to sleep like the dead. I know your life as a kid was rough, moving around, changing schools, and I was so proud that we could give you a place to live. I felt like that's what made me and my mom and my town a good place. I know it's stupid now—when you're a kid, you want the things you have to be the best. I was so happy to have you in my house, Peter. I wanted to give you the best.

And I really thought I had. I mean, I know school was tough on you. We tried to make it better, but you were just... you didn't give a fuck if anyone knew who you were or what you were. It was such amazing courage. I don't know where it came from. And all that bullshit—it seemed like a small price to pay. I think about it now, and me and Bodi, we could have been living in Arcata that whole time, and nobody would have known or cared, but we wanted to be there for Juliet and for you. THAT was a small price to pay. Living somewhere that made us all feel like it was okay for me and Bodi to beat the hell out of little juvenile delinquents so you'd be safe? That was a really big price. That was blood from all of us. That wasn't the thing I was proud of when I watched you sleep when you were little. How did I not know that?

I don't know why it hit me tonight. To be honest, this night was nothing new—but suddenly I realized I hadn't seen you in six years. Six years. God, Peter—you were only with us for six years, and that's how long I've been gone? And I realize you're still sending your mail from Daisy, and I want to know why the hell you haven't left there by now.

So this is me, your cousin who still loves you even though you might find it hard to believe. I'm telling you to get the hell out of that town. Being made to feel like shit because of who you love, that's no way to live. It wrecked me and Bodi, made me feel like we shouldn't be together, made him feel like he killed his sister, just… just fucking wrecked us. I even came back, thinking he could fix me, but the truth is, I just broke him more. I have so little faith in anything now, Peter. About the only thing I know for certain is that you and Bodi, you were the best of us. I broke him, and you need to get out of that fucking town before it does the same thing to you.

If you see Bodi, don't tell him who I am anymore. Don't tell him that I'm the platoon in-box, don't tell him I never quit my bad habits—he'll know what that means. Tell him he's better off without me, and then keep driving. I sent my mom money for your schooling—thinking about it now, I maybe should have just sent it to you. I trusted her my whole life to love me—it's a hard habit to get over, and if she's been keeping the money I sent, and that's why you haven't left yet, I'm sorry.

Just know that when I left Daisy behind I left you behind, and Daisy can kiss my ass, but I loved you, Peter—you were the best little brother a guy could have. I think of you like that, like my little brother, and whether I come back from this place or not, or this last tour ever ends or not, I want you to know that. When I was young and stupid and innocent, I loved you, and now that I'm not any of that shit anymore, I still love you. And I still love Bodi too, dammit, but thinking about that only hurts. Thinking about you—it's about the one good thing I've got left, so do me a favor and don't fuck it up by writing back to tell me what a fucker I am for leaving, okay? I mean, you haven't said that yet—but you should have, and now I'm hoping you don't.

And it's late and my body hurts and we might see shit tomorrow and I can't make myself care. But here, in the dark of the barracks, I just keep thinking about you sleeping, and how I thought you were safe, and how it was a lie and we never knew it, none of us knew it, until the end right there.

I want you to be safe, little brother. I want you to be happy. Please, when you write me again, tell me you're both, okay?

Michael

Peter stood up blindly after an hour, the top of his T-shirt sopping wet, his head aching, everything in his body hurting with his cousin's last words to him. His nose gave a weak throb, and he was shocked by that. Hadn't it been months since that happened? Years? A lifetime? He had no idea what would be in Michael's *real* last letter. He hoped Aileen took some solace from it, because Peter wouldn't read it. This was the only letter from his cousin he would ever need to read, and it was horrible but it was wonderful too.

You wonder. You lose faith. Michael loved him. And not all of the Michael that Peter had loved had died six years ago. Some of it had been left, and the rest?

Well, that was on Daisy's head, wasn't it.

Peter moved restlessly, pulling his books off shelves and stacking them into neat piles, pulling Michael's CDs off the shelf, putting them in a pile of their own. He closed his laptop on the small wooden desk that had been in the room when he'd arrived, wound up the cord, and started throwing clothes to shove in his duffle bag on the bed.

He made two trips down to the garage for boxes, and then four trips down to his car, which he locked securely in the driveway so Aileen could have the garage.

When he was done, he was left in the room with one good suit of clothes, a sleep shirt and some boxers, and the letter Aileen had left him lying on top of the one Michael had left.

What the hell—while the first blood was fresh, right?

There were two pieces of paper in the envelope, and one of them was a check.

Peter—

This here is money from the last couple checks Michael sent me. I hadn't given it to the church yet. I don't know just why.

For six years I was angry at you—it was like your kind took my son away. Maybe I was just too hurt to see I sent him away myself.

*I'm sorry I was not the mother I should have
been, and not the person either of you needed. If
it's any consolation, long after you're gone, I'll be
hearing the two of you talk through your wall, like
you did at night when you thought I couldn't hear.
I've been hearing it for six years. I don't know
why I should stop now.*

*Regret is the sound of the ghosts of our own
making. I will live with mine until I die.*

*I do love you in my way. And I'm sorry about
the Kovacs boy. If you can stand to, visit
sometime. I'd like that. I'm about done with what
people here think anyway.*

    Aileen

Peter was wept dry by that time. He couldn't think about it anymore. He couldn't think about all that Aileen could have had and never would now. He couldn't think about his beautiful cousin and the emptiness his life had been after he'd left. He couldn't even think about Bodi and how there was still hope. He was weary, to every last pore in his skin, weary and heartsore and used.

He simply stretched out on his bed and thought of one of Bodi's paintings, one of the bright ones, with sunlight and grasses and a blue sea. He remembered the sound from the edge of the highway, when he and Bodi had been looking out at the surf, and the smell of salt that never quite went away. He was there, in the painting, the sun on his face, Bodi's hand in his, when he fell asleep.

Sometime in the night he had a waking dream, the sort you have when you're too tired to wake yourself up when you know it's not real. He dreamt that he and Michael were kids again, and Michael, who slept on the other side of the wall, got his attention by knocking softly and whispering to him.

"Hey, Peter, you awake?"

"Am now."

"Can I tell you something?"

"Yeah."

"I'm in love."

"With who?"

"Bodi Kovacs."

"But Michael, I love him too."

A beat of silence.

"He was mine first, Peter."

"But you can't take care of him. He needs to be cared for."

"I'm the oldest. You know that. I'm the oldest, so I can do it best."

He woke in the morning with an aching head and a heart boiling in its own blood.

I AM THE RESURRECTION
AND THE LIFE

IT WAS funny, the differences in perception that people had.

Everyone in town—even Bodi and Michael—thought that Peter's years growing up with his mother had been seven slices of hell, but that's not what Peter remembered.

Sure, they'd moved around a lot, and no, meals hadn't been regular. But Peter's mother had been... well, she'd been young, for one thing.

She had played. She had sent him cards for his birthdays and showed up sometimes for Christmases, although not so much in later years, and she always told him to have fun. "Are you having fun, baby? Go out and play for me, okay?"

When Peter remembered being a child, he remembered her taking him to the park a lot, and to the zoo, and sneaking him into movies when they couldn't afford to pay, which was always. He remembered her taking him to the library and reading Shel Silverstein books just to make him giggle. He remembered impromptu games of tag and how getting food stamps was cause for celebration and how even when they were eating white rice and ketchup or peanut butter and jelly for a month, there was always, somehow, enough money for a three-penny piece of candy at the grocery store.

Of course now, as a grown up, he realized that she must have stolen some of that candy, but God. Back then?

It had made his world.

He'd cried when she told him she was taking him to Aunt Aileen's. He remembered that day so clearly.

"Baby… I'm so sorry." Her hair back then had been dyed black, with a brassy blonde streak through the temple and back, and it fell in loose, tangled curls down the front of her peasant blouse. The last month had been particularly rough on them both. They'd had to move again, because her job had changed hours and she just didn't make enough to keep rent, and someone had stolen the food stamps out of her purse when she'd been at the unemployment office. She'd gone out on a date, though, and although she'd cried afterward, she'd had enough food for them both the next day, and Peter thought they'd been doing okay.

But she'd gone out on another date after that, and this one had gone badly. She had a bruise on her cheek when she got home, and even though Peter had brought her ice, she'd still put her face in her arms and cried some more.

But she'd always sworn she'd never take Peter to Daisy. He'd heard her say it often enough to friends when he'd been smaller, and to him as he'd gotten big enough to talk. "Yeah, it's tough, Petey— but not as bad as Daisy. We'll know shit's really bad when I take you back there."

The year before, when he was nine, he'd confided quietly to her (because it was the two of them, it was always the two of them, and until Michael, there was no one else in his life that he'd rather talk to) that he'd wanted to kiss boys instead of girls and asked her if that was okay. She'd started to cry then and told him that of course it was okay. Of course it was okay—but that it wasn't okay in Daisy, and that's why they couldn't go.

But Aileen had sent Ginnifer Armbruster Christmas cards and pictures too, and Peter knew that Aileen had a son. When things got hard, when they were down to white rice and ketchup and powdered milk, when the heat got turned off and he and his mother had to huddle under blankets on the bed, or when the lease expired and they were living out of a car and bathing in the river, Peter would ask them why they couldn't go to Daisy.

"It sounds like a flower, Mom. Aren't flowers supposed to be beautiful?"

And Ginnifer would look at him sorrowfully. "They're supposed to be, baby. They are. But this one only looks pretty. Inside there's a poison, Petey. It won't kill you outright, but if you stay there too long, your heart will just shrivel up and die."

She really had been a pretty woman when Peter was younger, with the same dark-fringed blue eyes that Peter had, and a feminine heart shape to her face much like the masculine heart shape that Peter grew into. He loved to look at her when she smiled, because her eyes weren't sad that way, and she'd always bent down and looked at him eye to eye, because it was just the two of them and they were in this together. "I want to see if maybe I can keep you from that sort of poison, okay? I've got a new job—maybe this one will have enough hours."

But it never did. She would work hard, but there were never enough hours for health insurance, and the lines in the social service places were so long, and food stamps never really seemed to fill the empty places. The month where Mom had to have two dates in a week—that seemed to be the deciding moment for her.

She cried the whole way on the bus, holding him on her lap like a little kid. "I'm sorry," she whispered. "I'm sorry." And then she proceeded to tell him the cost that he'd have to pay for a bed and a roof and three meals a day.

He would have to either keep who he wanted to kiss to himself, or he would have to be brave about it. He told her he'd be brave. He would have to not swear and not contradict the grown-ups.

He said this would be harder to do.

"I know, baby," she laughed. Peter often made sure his mother had her purse or her keys and helped her remember when the month started because she wasn't good at that, and they'd lost more than one apartment not because she didn't have money but because she forgot to pay the rent. Peter was used to being treated like a grown-up.

"You're going to have to just watch the grown-ups around you make mistakes in this place," Ginnifer told him. "Otherwise they'll think you're a bad kid, and I'm not doing this so you can grow up like that."

"Anything else?" he asked, not sure he shouldn't just make her turn the bus around. (Or maybe, he thought seriously, just get off at a stop not a place that seemed to cause his mother so much pain.)

"Yeah," she sighed, looking out the window, maybe so he wouldn't have to see her eyes. "You're going to have to go to church."

"What's church?"

"It's a place where you dress up—"

"I'd like that! Clean clothes?" Clean clothes were a luxury then.

"Yeah. Clean clothes."

"Then maybe it's not so bad."

His mother's mouth tightened. "Honey, they're going to tell you all sorts of stuff that's going to sound really good. They're going to tell you Bible stories—"

"Like the men at the shelter?" Yeah. They'd spent a Christmas there once. It hadn't smelled great, and it had been crowded, but Peter had gotten new clothes that fit and an action figure. All in all, not completely horrible, but he'd still enjoyed the Christmas after that when they'd had a small apartment and, on Christmas Eve, their own tree.

"Yeah," Ginnifer said, sighing like adults did when stuff was hard for little kids to understand. "Like the men at the shelter. At church they'll tell you these stories about Jesus, and don't get me wrong, he was a really good man. But be careful, Peter. The people telling the stories don't always act like him."

Peter mulled this over for a minute. He'd liked the stories—they'd had passion and drama and excitement. Who wouldn't like a story like that? He was trying to figure out what the warning was about.

"Like how?"

Again, that sigh. "Like, Jesus says things like 'judge not, lest ye be judged', right?"

"Yeah."

"Well, these people at the church, they're going to be looking at you the whole time, judging, weighing, trying to decide if you're good enough to be in the church. And if you're not, they'll make sure you feel so completely shitty, you'll never want to come back."

Peter looked at her, still puzzled. "But if they're mean to you, why would you want to go back?"

Ginnifer started to cry. "Because it's hard, Peter. It's so hard to be on your own. It's hard when you don't know when your next meal is coming from, or if you don't have a place to stay. I want you to feel safe, baby." She folded her arms around Peter's shoulders, and Peter let her. "I'm just never sure if the cost is worth it, you know?"

He didn't know. He didn't.

And then he'd arrived on Aileen's porch, holding his mother's hand so tightly it must have hurt, but she never complained. Aileen had smiled at him tentatively, but he'd remembered. He remembered his mother telling him to watch out when people in this town smiled, so he nodded gravely at her and said thank you when she took them in for sandwiches.

He'd stayed that way, grave and wide-eyed, until Michael had run into the kitchen and grabbed him by the hand. "Mom, can he come play?"

"Sure, Michael, what are you doing?"

"Some kid got a motorbike—we're taking it apart because something's wrong with it." This was a year or so before Bodi, and the identity of "some kid" was lost forever in Peter's memory. But that was okay. "Some kid" left, and it was just Michael asking Peter to hand him things and telling him about motorcycles and that holy of holies, the Harley Davidson.

They were working away when Peter's mom came to the garage to say good-bye.

Peter remembered being stricken. He'd been having fun. It had been ages since he'd played with a boy his age, and even though Michael was older, he'd been as excited to have a cousin as Peter had been. They'd compared hair color, eye color, height, face shape, strengths, and weaknesses. Peter was smarter. Michael said that from the very beginning. Michael was more beautiful. Peter had thought it, but he didn't have the words. So he'd felt bad, guilty, that he'd enjoyed Michael's company so much, and that he'd forgotten. He'd forgotten, and his mother was leaving, and he couldn't change it.

He'd run to her unabashedly and clung, not even trying not to cry.

"It's only for a little while," she murmured, but he knew that sound in her voice by now. *It's only a date, Peter. He'll buy us some food, it'll be fine. It's okay about the job, Peter, there's another one waiting. If they can't deal with the fact that I've got a kid hanging out after school, then fuck 'em.*

"It's only for a little while," she said again. "Just until I can bring us home some happy." He'd cried harder then, because they both knew it was a lie.

So his mother had left, and his last memory of her until Christmas had been watching her shoulders shaking as she'd walked toward Daisy's small bus depot, and he was suddenly surprised by Michael's hand on his shoulder.

"It's okay, Peter," Michael said earnestly. "We'll take care of you. Honest. It's a real good place. We'll go to church tomorrow, it'll be good. Church is boring as hell, of course, but the women get together and make snack—it'll be fine. You'll like Daisy, Peter. You will."

That night, he'd been crying in his bed, so softly he thought nobody could hear him. There had been a gentle knock on his wall.

"Peter?"

"Yeah?"

"You okay in there?"

Sniffle. "Yeah. Fine."

"It's okay if you miss her. I'd miss my mom too."

"She doesn't want to go," Peter said, and as an adult, looking back at that moment, Peter was proud that he still believed it.

"I know she didn't," Michael soothed. "Did you have your own room before?"

"No," Peter said back, because that was almost frightening too.

"Well, pretend that she's in the next room, okay? I'll be here. If you wake up, just knock, and I'll knock back, and you can think it's her."

That was how he'd slept so well in the first months. When he was asleep, he could pretend his mother was in the living room, looking at want ads, while he slept in their bedroom, because a one bedroom was all they'd ever been able to afford.

In later months, he slept well because he knew it was Michael there, and because Michael would protect him like his mother could not.

AND now he sat in Daisy's biggest building, its church, and remembered that day. The church was big and square and unapologetic, with a bell tower and small vestibule next to the pulpit and a small kitchen and day-care room connected by doors to the bulk of the building. It was painted white inside and out, and there were stained glass windows, the big mural kind with the arches in the tops, depicting the various stages of the Crucifixion of Christ. Peter had driven past the churches in Arcata before. They had stained glass windows showing the Sermon on the Mount and walking on water and the birth, but not Daisy. Daisy had the blood and the whipping and the body wrapped in a shroud at the tomb.

Peter could remember that first day, sitting next to Michael, dressed in Michael's hand-me-down church clothes since he hadn't had any of his own, and supposedly listening to the sermon. What he'd heard, loud and clear, were his mother's words on the bus.

Well, these people at the church, they're going to be looking at you the whole time, judging, weighing, trying to decide if you're good enough to be in the church. And if you're not, they'll make sure you feel so completely shitty, you'll never want to come back.

Just looking at those windows, he thought, *This must be their favorite part of the story. The part where somebody bleeds.*

Nothing that had happened since that day had led him to feel any different.

He sat at the end of the first pew—where family was supposed to sit—and tried not to look at the big coffin draped in the American flag while he waited for his Aunt Aileen to disembark from the limousine. She'd asked him, actually, if he wanted to ride with her, since the town was helping to front the funeral expenses, and he'd declined, but not bitterly.

"I'm driving there," he said apologetically. "That way I can just leave when the funeral is over."

Aileen's tight, stoic expression weakened for a moment, and Peter... well, given what Peter had planned, he actually felt something in his chest ease up. He could afford some forgiveness in him now, because he knew she'd never be able to forgive him for what he had in mind.

He came close enough to her to hold out his arms in question, and she took a step in. He gave her a brief, awkward hug.

"I'll just be in Arcata," he said quietly. "I'll have the same cell phone. You can call me from the landline, and I'll get it."

She nodded and looked at him uncertainly. "What should I tell your mother?"

God. The last time he'd seen her... well, she'd looked older than forty, which is all she'd been. He grimaced. "Tell her that if she needs it, and if she's clean, I can make a home for her."

Aileen nodded and looked around the small house that she'd always kept neat and plain, even when Michael blew through it, leaving puddles of clothes and schoolbooks and life.

"If you don't mind," she said apologetically, "I'll ask her to stay with me first." She swallowed. "I never asked her, when she came to drop you off. I made it sound like it was too much trouble." A knock sounded at the door, and Aileen was so lost in memory that she didn't even startle. "It shouldn't have been too much trouble." She wiped her eyes with the back of her hand composedly and then turned around to the front door.

"Good-bye, Peter," she said softly. "I hope you and that Kovacs boy, you find some happy."

"Thanks for the college money," he said, and she nodded, still facing away.

"A little bit of right in a whole lot of wrong. See you at the church."

She left, and he took the last of his things from his room and walked away with one last look. It was his last good-bye to Michael, really, because what he planned to say at the funeral, that was a whole different thing.

So Peter stood in the pew as the coffin was borne into the tiny church by men from the town with an army officer on either side, one to play the recording of "Taps" and one to present the flag. Apparently this had been planned without him, and he experienced a moment of petty anger—shouldn't he get to be a pallbearer? But then he remembered the day before, the way he and Bodi had watched Michael's beloved Harley Davidson burn to a blackened frame in the canyon, and thought that maybe it would be good to

161

remember what Michael would have wanted and what he wouldn't have given a royal shit about.

The pews filled, and Peter put his hand in his pocket and felt for the bowie knife Michael had given him when he was fourteen, fiddled with it, looked at the little program for the service, and tried to firm up his plan.

He looked long and hard at the American flag and decided that maybe that wasn't the way to go. No. He'd wait until God had said his piece and then tell the world what he thought. He'd leave the government out of it—for now.

There was a cloth on the pulpit with the same insignia as the Christian flag. It had a little red cross in a field of blue against that dazzling background of can't-be-wrong virginal white, and Peter thought that would do just fine. The whole town looked at the word that came down from that place like it really was God's word—maybe it was time they saw that the men who spoke up there were just as fallible as Michael and Peter and Bodi. Maybe it was time they saw that the hate that seemed to come from that place, regardless of who stood there, was human, and not from God at all.

Everybody stood for the invocation, and everybody except Peter put his head down in humility as the pastor led the little church in prayer. Everybody opened the hymnal and sang "Nearer, My God, to Thee," and everybody except Peter opened their mouths and tried to give grace to the old words and even older tune. Everybody sat when the pastor began to speak about Michael and how he had strayed from the flock for a while, but how his service to his country proved that he had come home to God at last, and everybody except Peter nodded their heads and accepted that it was so.

Peter sat in the pew and looked up at the flag-draped coffin with burning eyes, his hand in his pocket fumbling with the knife, until the pastor asked if anyone would like to speak.

Peter stood up then, the murmured hush of the assembly—a good three hundred people, including a crowd at the open door and standing along the walls, fanning themselves in the press of bodies—lost in the sudden bite of the knife across his palm.

He opened his mouth with every intention of just letting his words fly when the unmistakable roar of a Harley Davidson cut through the open door.

Peter jerked his head toward the church entrance, and that murmur grew louder, more intense, more upset, and outraged as the Harley cut off in mid-roar. For the first time in twenty-four hours, Peter felt something besides emptiness and grief pounding in his chest.

The crowd parted then, and in he walked, wearing his good black riding leathers and with a helmet dangling from each hand. The entire church assembly turned to watch him.

He apparently didn't give a fuck about them, because he searched the crowd restlessly until he saw Peter up front, and even though he grimaced in embarrassment, it couldn't change the fact that the impossible had just happened.

Bodi Kovacs had just come home.

COMING HOME

PETER actually felt tears for the first time that day, but the smile he turned toward Bodi as he stood in the front of the church was as full of all his heart as any he'd given in his life.

Bodi's eyes darted left to right as he walked forward, but his shoulders were squared and he kept his face turned toward Peter the whole time. As he got close enough to speak, even the quietest murmurs in the back of the church faded. Oh yeah. Everyone wanted to hear what Peter Armbruster and Bodi Kovacs had to say.

Peter didn't really give a shit what they wanted. Bodi had come home.

"I thought you said you weren't coming?" Peter said, but the corners of his mouth were pulling up, and he was fighting the urge to just throw his arms around Bodi's neck and cling like he'd never clutched another human being to his heart before, not even his mother.

Bodi didn't answer immediately. Instead, he cupped Peter's chin between his gloved thumb and forefinger and held Peter in place for a sweet and gentle kiss, right there, literally in front of God and everybody.

"I don't want you to leave, I gotta make myself someone worth staying for," he said as he pulled back. He looked around again at the shocked and titillated assembly, his shoulders twitching as the outraged whispers started. "Uhm... maybe I should sit down."

Peter shook his head and put his clean hand up to feather across his tingling lips. Oh God yes. Bodi Kovacs was *so* worth staying for. "I was just about to speak anyway, and then we can leave, okay?"

For a moment Bodi's shoulders sagged and his face lit up in relief, and then someone in the back pew whispered "Faggots!" and he straightened up and grimaced. "Okay, then," he muttered. "You speak."

"Come with me," Peter said, tucking the helmet under his arm and reaching out with his clean hand to clutch at Bodi's. Bodi looked behind him forlornly, met the eyes of that damning crowd, and looked back at Peter, shaking his head.

"Like I'm going to sit down alone here?" he muttered and dutifully followed Peter as Peter took the steps up to the dais.

There were more whispers then, and Peter gave Bodi his helmet before he looked out at the assembly and pulled his hand out of his pocket. He spread his fingers and opened it in demonstration.

It was covered in blood.

The wound wasn't deep and it wasn't dripping, but it crossed the scar Peter had from when he'd fallen on the saw in the garage, and suddenly there weren't any whispers in the church anymore, there was only shock.

"Michael's blood is on the hands of everyone here," he said brutally, and then he squeezed Bodi's hand, because Bodi had grunted in shock too.

"Young man, this is a funeral—"

Peter turned toward the pastor, who hadn't been there six years before, but it didn't matter. "This isn't your business," he said shortly, and the man—older, probably planning to retire in Daisy— took a step back from the venom in Peter's voice.

"Six years ago, a really shitty thing happened," he said, and he looked Bodi's mother full on in the face. She looked older too, but she had Juliet's and Bodi's blue eyes and sandy-blonde hair. She glared defiantly back at Peter like he was accusing her of something, and he shook his head. "It was awful. I cried for Juliet Kovacs—I did. I missed her. I helped Bodi care for her, and she was my friend. But Bodi and his mom? They did the best they could. They watched her every minute of every day. They were *exhausted* with the watching of her—you all knew that. So Bodi gave Ashley Eschenger some money to watch his sister while he got away for a while."

Ashley Eschenger was Ashley Drescher now, and she had been pretty and blonde and happy when she was twenty years old. Now she was just like Aileen and Joelle and Judy—old at the eyes and mouth when she didn't need to be, and like Joelle, she was plump with too much motherhood too early. She didn't look Peter in the face. She was sitting with her youngest—not yet a year old, it looked like—in her arms, and after grimacing at Peter like she couldn't bear to see him, she looked down into the face of her child. Peter quirked his mouth at her, seeing the once blonde hair now a dirty-dishwater color, the coarsening of the lines in her face on her neck. Her mouth, which had once been open and smiling, was compressed and flat now, and she sat next to Warren like he had all the appeal of a rotting corpse. She must have felt horrible. Warren was looking off to the side like none of this had anything to do with him, and neither of them had dealt with what had happened and forgiven themselves for it. Well, that was not Peter's fault.

"So they took a break, that's all," Peter said, pulling himself away from the two of them. "And you all were fine with that. You didn't give a shit what he was doing. You thought that was okay, that he got to have some time to not worry." Peter squeezed Bodi's hand and looked at him, and Bodi looked away.

"It would have been great too," Peter said, thinking that his chest and his throat felt freer than he'd expected. He'd been afraid he'd get up and do nothing but scream or cry, but he was speaking, and his voice was carrying, and it felt good. "But Ashley…." He bit back bitter words. "Ashley wasn't prepared, really, and Juliet…." His eyes found Judy Kovacs again, and she looked away through one of the stained glass panels, her mouth shaking in sorrow. "Juliet was damned determined. And that was bad. That was fucking awful. But it should have been the end of it. It should have. This town should have mourned for Juliet, but instead…." Peter shook his head.

"How could you?" he asked, and there was a shocked, uncomfortable silence in return. "How could all of you put the blame for something like that on Bodi and Michael—have you asked yourselves that? What they were doing—"

"Fucking faggots!" someone shouted from the back of the church.

"Was none of your fucking business!" Peter shouted, and nobody replied. "But you used it anyway, didn't you? You treated it like it was all their fault. You drove Bodi out of town, and Michael...."

Peter shook his head and wiped at his eyes with the back of his hand. "You told him that the only way to atone for his sins was death, didn't you? I heard you. I heard all of you. You said better dead than a fag. Well, people. Here he is. I hope you're proud of yourselves. He didn't die for his country. He died for you."

Peter walked deliberately up the steps and past Michael's coffin to the pulpit in front of the preacher. He looked at that cloth, embroidered and starched by the good women of Daisy, and hesitated. Some part of him was still the wide-eyed boy who wanted to honor all the things the adults told him were good.

He looked at the coffin again.

Peter hadn't been that boy since his mother left. He hadn't been that boy when he watched the destruction of the two people he loved most. He wasn't that boy now. He put his bloody hand on that dazzling field of white and pressed, and then turned around to the baffled assembly.

"Juliet Kovacs's blood is no longer on Michael and Bodi's hands. And Michael's blood is on yours." He took two steps toward the steps and then realized Bodi was coming up, taking off his gloves as he walked. Peter looked at him in surprise.

"Give me the knife," Bodi muttered, and Peter did, taking Bodi's helmet along with his own while Bodi fumbled with it, and knowing his eyes were huge and his mouth was all but hanging open. Bodi was smarter than Peter had been; he sliced the top of his

the

hand, between his thumb and forefinger, where the cut wouldn't get in the way of anything he needed to do. Peter had cut his left hand and Bodi cut his right, and Peter caught the fact that Bodi, the quiet artist, was going for symmetry when he pulled the altar cloth flat and placed his own handprint next to Peter's.

Bodi turned around and saw that the eyes of the assembly were upon him, and Peter watched him swallow. They expected him to say something, and Bodi was not much of a public speaker. His throat worked again, and then he looked at that dark and damning coffin next to him. Peter watched Bodi's triangular jaw firm up, and his eyes blazed out at the pews full of churchgoers.

"My sister's death was *not* my fault," he snarled. "And I don't owe any of you people shit."

Peter felt the most absurd and powerful urge to laugh, but he didn't. He waited for Bodi to draw close, and he held the two helmets by their straps as he reached out his bloodied hand to Bodi's, and Bodi took it. The blood was sticky and visceral, and they looked each other in the eye without flinching before they both turned and walked out of the church.

Aileen was sobbing as they walked by, but she shook off Joelle's embrace enough to wave at them in blessing. Peter caught Nate's quiet wave as they neared the back of the church, and he nodded. Nate smiled like he'd won something, and Peter thought that maybe he'd found a friend he'd thought he lost. But other than that, the crowd was quiet, shaken, and, oddly enough, respectful of them. The crowd at the door parted to let them out. Neither of them looked back.

When they cleared the crowd, nobody followed them, and Peter led Bodi around the side of the church, where giant planted oak trees shaded the west side of the building and kept it cool. That was the side where they had ice cream socials in the summer, and that was the side closest to the river. When they reached the brown-and-green shade, Peter tugged Bodi past the parking lot and behind the church, shivering but still determined.

They came to the river—the same river they had spent the week in near the swimming hole upstream, the same river that washed the dead animals in its inlets, and the same river that washed out to the ocean. The sound of this river was the quiet chorus behind every sermon and the elemental music behind every hymn. This morning, it sparkled in the sunlight before it ran to the soft bank at their feet, and Peter dropped their helmets on the giving, mossy earth and squatted down. He took off his one white dress shirt, which left him in his white tank and black slacks, and swished the sleeve of it in the river. When he was done, he took Bodi's hand in his own. He washed Bodi off, his own blood staining and dissipating into the river in the process, and used the dry part of the shirt to wipe their hands. Neither of the cuts were deep, and they had stopped bleeding after being shocked with the cold. When they were both clean and dry, Peter took Bodi's hand in his own and brought the back of it to his lips.

Bodi closed his eyes, and when he opened them, he smiled, his eyes as bright and as blue as the dazzling spring sky reflected in the river behind him.

"You came back," Peter said again, and that smile grew wider.

"You're worth it."

"You stood up with me."

"Did I mention the first part?" Bodi was laughing softly, and Peter's chest was coiled like a steel spring, there was so much joy behind it.

"You know," Peter said, trying to be conversational, "you're the only person who's ever fought for me, right?"

Bodi blinked. "Michael—"

"Left. But I forgive him for that because you came back."

Bodi's teasing smile faded, became serious, and he leaned forward, taking Peter's chin in his hands again and kissing him softly. "If that's all it takes?" he said when he pulled back. "The coming back for you? If that's all it takes to keep you? I can do that, Peter. I can *always* come back for you."

169

Peter let that joy shine through in his smile and stood up, offering Bodi his hand. Bodi took his hand and hauled himself to his feet, and Peter used his momentum and pulled him into his arms. Their mouths met, and this kiss was for real, for long, the good kind between two people who had just declared their love in front of God.

They pulled apart, and Peter squinted back over the river. Downstream was a footbridge that led to the cemetery, and he imagined that the honor guard and whichever men Aileen had culled from the town would cross it later that day and bear Michael's body to its resting place. A part of him mourned that he and Bodi wouldn't have a part of that, but most of him? Most of him knew that what he and Bodi had done the day before had been far more powerful, and that it was something that only the three of them would have understood.

In his head, Peter said a quiet, final good-bye to his cousin. *I love you, Michael. I'll try to remember you lying next to my room and telling me it's all right.*

Peter's gaze traveled back over the river and to the stretch of woods and the church again. From this angle he should have been able to see the Toyota, and he couldn't.

"Bodi, where's my car?"

Bodi grinned like this was the best surprise ever. "Shawn's got it."

"Got it how?"

"Got it, hot-wired it. It's an old car, Peter, it wasn't hard."

Peter could only stare at him, not even bothering to hold back his amusement. "Jesus, Bodi—my car! Everything I own is in there!"

Bodi nodded happily. "We noticed that. That's why she's taking it back to my place. By the time we get to Arcata, after stopping for dinner and all, her kids'll probably have it all moved in."

Peter blinked. "You planned this."

Bodi nodded, his eyes actually dancing. "If I'm not broken, Peter, I can take care of shit on my own." The breeze kicked up, and he smiled, those asymmetrical blue eyes seeking out the direction of it, and he tilted his face up to the wind. "Do you feel that?" he asked, closing his eyes happily. "It's like it's calling us, isn't it?"

Peter nodded, his own eyes still fixed hungrily on Bodi's face. "Yeah," he whispered hoarsely. He moved closer to Bodi, wrapped his arm around Bodi's waist, and shivered at the sudden chill.

Bodi put an arm protectively around his shoulders and held him. "C'mon, Petey. It's calling us home."

Peter nodded, but he still had no words, none at all.

Bodi picked up the helmets at their feet and then started toward the parking lot, keeping Peter tucked securely under his arm. He followed Bodi to the bike and took a look around. The preacher was thundering something inside the church, and the attention of the entire town was focused inward, so they were the only two people in the world of Daisy.

"Bye, Daisy," he said softly, and Bodi grunted.

"Hello, Arcata, and aren't you a crazy asshole to think that's a step up."

Peter managed a smile. "You're there, Bodi. It's home."

The ride home was long, but Peter got to lean against Bodi's back for much of it and hold on tight, so it seemed to go damned quick. The wind from the road blew the last of Daisy from his face, from his thoughts, from his heart, and when he and Bodi got to Arcata, he felt brand-new and clean, ready to walk hand in hand into a future with Bodi, baptized by the sea.

EPILOGUE
A YEAR IN YOUR ARMS

GOD, he was tired. He was tired and his body hurt from working late in the garage with Bodi the night before, and his brain hurt from the finals that had just finished the *week* before, and his eyeballs hurt from the sun streaming into Bodi's bedroom at some sort of obscene morning hour when sun would be better off hiding behind clouds.

He moaned and pulled the quilt over his head. It was a new quilt, something he'd bought with the salary Bodi paid him from his work in the garage. He liked it—there was a little quilt store nearby, and he'd picked the colors of Bodi's pictures. Blues and greens and soft golds, punctuated by flashes of fiery orange and red. It was peaceful and passionate together, like the ocean and the sun and Bodi. He loved it a lot, but right now, not even that quilt and the sheets and blankets underneath it were thick enough to keep the sun out.

And it didn't help that Bodi was just lying there on his side of the bed, looking at Peter patiently with those hopeful blue eyes.

"What?" Peter growled. Not too loudly, though. This last year, he had learned to be careful with Bodi.

Bodi wasn't really broken anymore, but sometimes he was fragile, and Peter had needed to learn as much about him as possible to make their first year together work.

Bodi was happiest in the shop, where his hands and his brain engaged in patterns sanded smooth by communal use. He worked well with Shawn and with Peter when Peter came in to help, but he was used to being a solitary creature, and Peter had come to respect that. Their walks in the evening, every evening, even if Peter had to leave a study session early or never even *think* of night classes in his schedule, were quiet, but Bodi needed them. The one time Peter had stayed late for a study group, he'd come back to find Bodi still in the shop, taking apart a motorcycle that he'd just put back together and making a list.

"Go shopping, Peter likes the cinnamon cereal, ask Shawn to order the parts, she already ordered the parts, ask her when they're coming in, dust the apartment, don't forget to paint tomorrow night, Peter will be there tomorrow night, I can paint."

They'd been living together for three months by then, getting up, eating breakfast, doing normal things, making love like sex-crazed lemmings at night. Until that moment Peter had never suspected that Bodi was still a little thin in places, might always be a little fragile. Peter heard his voice mumbling that dreaded list, and he realized that once he had inserted himself into Bodi's life, he needed to be very, very careful about changing the pattern of how Bodi had been put back together after being broken. Even for a study group, or which nights they went out for dinner (Tuesdays), or when they woke up (seven on most days, nine on the weekends), things had to be regular. Peter had needed to learn that Bodi had been *very* much alone, and that he had survived without his family, without his friends, without his lover, by making sure his days were ordered, predictable, and regulated like the ticking of the clock. It was the reason he could come home and get high that first night Peter had knocked on the door—getting high was in his mental schedule under "things I can do after the walk and before I go to bed." (Peter had since *removed* that item from the schedule, but it helped to understand how Bodi's mind worked.)

So Peter had needed to accept responsibility. He'd told Bodi he'd always be there, which meant he'd needed to give up things like night classes or day trips somewhere when Bodi couldn't make it. It was only fair, since Bodi's life had expanded to fit him, and Peter's life since he'd moved in?

Peter's life had grown in ways he'd never even thought of.

He was loved when he woke up. He was touched when he fell asleep at night. He held someone close and laughed at television or shared his books. Living with Bodi was warm because Bodi—whether he was brushing by Peter from behind or hugging him or fucking him into the bed—was just as starved for touch as Peter, and they would clasp skin until it warmed under fingers, and fingers warmed to their touch. Bodi would not go walking without Peter now that they had shared that first walk. He would spend hours of their Sunday off painting or reading slowly and listening to music while Peter read or worked on his studies, and at least once an hour, he would walk by and rub his cheek on the back of Peter's head or, if his hands weren't covered in paint or paint remover, he would clasp Peter's hand in passing, gradually letting it go as he walked out of range. He wouldn't speak when he did this, but then, he didn't have to. They had touched, Bodi had a human in his house, a pack to answer to. He was happy, he was safe, he was loved.

It was... wonderful. Not perfect, of course, but truly, truly wonderful. Peter watched sometimes when Bodi lapsed into moody silences that lasted for days. Sometimes Peter would wake up and look at him, his longish sandy-brown/blond hair in a mess on his pillow, his mouth slightly parted in sleep, as innocent as a sunny day, and think *I've stolen this. This was Michael's.* But Bodi would come out of his silences as long as Peter stayed constant by his side, and when Bodi opened his eyes in the morning, he was never looking for Michael. Ever.

That September they celebrated Michael's birthday for the first time in seven years. They sat on the beach and got roaring drunk until dawn, and then walked home, bleary and teary and ready to fall into bed together, not to make love, just to keep telling that one last story about Michael's childhood until neither of them could remember who stopped and who fell asleep in the middle of a sentence.

The next day Peter started school, and the world became new.

It was funny, though—at least Peter thought so. He was going to college, and the work was a challenge, and the things he learned were interesting. He loved all of his classes, the accounting ones and the humanities ones and the college-level astronomy and physics of course, but...

But as much as he was pretty sure his horizons were expanded, he didn't have any urge to go farther than Arcata without Bodi by his side. Yeah, sure, he'd love to see the world. But he found that simple things—the perfect puzzle that was putting together a motorcycle, the exact shape of the shoreline near their home as it altered from day to day, the way Bodi looked at him sometimes when he thought Peter wasn't looking, with his eyes focused and his lean mouth turned up at the corners, the way it had been in high school—*these* simple things were all he needed to live. In fact, they made his life full.

The two of them had friends too. Shawn and her family were constants in their lives. Shawn had them over to dinner at least twice a month, and Peter and Bodi got to know her taciturn husband, big strapping sons, and her tiny, delicate daughter who was taken to ballet twice a week and treated like a princess by the men in her life, which included Peter and Bodi. Peter remembered Lucy and Bodi's quiet joy that she had stayed in the garage and talked to him.

Sometimes he came home from class and found Darien sitting on her little stool, still wearing her school clothes, doing her homework while her mother worked on cars, and thought that Bodi had done a first-class job of finding some family on his own.

Peter made friends from school, and since he didn't like to stay out late studying, he was pleased when two of them—Heidi and Alex—started coming over to their place to crash on their couch.

That Christmas, between Christmas and New Year's, Peter's mother came to stay. Aunt Aileen drove her—she'd apparently stayed at Aileen's for Christmas Eve and Christmas Day—but she slept on Peter and Bodi's couch for two days, and went walking on the beach with them, and saw Bodi's paintings, and visited with Shawn's family too.

She took Peter aside the morning Aileen came to get her, and held his face in her hands and kissed his cheek.

She looked younger now, and she still dyed most of her hair black instead of blonde, and her face was still heart shaped and her eyes were still that blue that was rimmed with black.

"You didn't let them tell you shit, did you, baby?" she asked quietly, and Peter bit his lip.

"I'm not as brave as I said I'd be," he confessed. "They almost got me. They almost got us both."

Her mouth had thinned a bit in later years, and she pursed it now. "Well, something you've done must have been good. Aileen asked me to come stay with her. This time, she said that church wasn't a requirement."

Peter smiled faintly at that. "Well, good for her. Are you going to?"

They were outside during this conversation, wrapped in parkas with gloves and hats and scarves, and Ginnifer grinned at him then and started down the stairs. They got to the bottom, and she started walking toward the roaring winter surf, which was visible down the block, and then she turned and made sure he was keeping up.

"I miss family," she confessed when he drew even with her. "Is that bad?"

Peter put an arm around her, and for the first time in all of her visits since that long-ago day twelve years before, he felt like she was his mom, really, and not the stranger who had come back in her place.

"Family is good for you," he said sincerely. "My life would be pretty damned empty if I didn't have Bodi."

Ginnifer sighed and rested her head against his arm. "My life was pretty damned empty when I left you."

Peter closed his eyes. "I missed you, Mom. If it hadn't been for Michael, I'm not sure I would have survived."

And he could say that now without bitterness or anger. Michael had been human after all, but that didn't mean he hadn't been a good human, and that didn't mean he hadn't kept Peter's heart intact when it might have shattered to dust.

Aileen showed up to get her sister the day after that, and to Peter's surprise, she got out of the car and hugged him. Family. Much like Bodi had been, Peter's family had been broken. Much like Bodi, it was trying to find the glue to stick together. Maybe, like Bodi, too, his little family would succeed, but whether it did or not, Peter was going to be fine.

Bodi was his family now.

So it was a good life, and a good time, and every morning when Peter got out of bed and realized he was in the little apartment above the motorcycle shop, he felt like the entire town of Daisy, with the disapproval and the suffocation, had been lifted off his shoulders.

He Facebooked with Nate every so often—and that was fine too.

So this morning, this fine, early June morning, he was ready to rest and call it sleep well earned, but Bodi…

Bodi was lying perpendicular to him with his chin propped in his hands and watching Peter like a kid watched his favorite cartoon.

"What?" Peter repeated groggily. "Isn't it early for Saturday?"

Bodi shook his head. "It's up."

Peter blinked at him. "What's up? The sun? Barely."

Bodi's glare couldn't hardly scare a seagull off the beach, and Peter was more charmed than frightened. "Your article, dumbshit! It's up on the site—and Peter, it's gotten about six hundred hits."

Peter scrambled out of bed so quickly he almost fell on the floor. His laptop was set up on a little computer desk behind the couch. Bodi had ordered the desk from Staples and then driven 150 miles in Shawn's truck to get it. It had been a back-to-school present, and Peter would never forget the pride on Bodi's face when he'd presented it, either. Peter's computer and school books were set up there, and when Peter stumbled through the little hall and into the living room, he saw that Bodi had booted up the website already. There was coffee brewing in the kitchen, but Peter was too focused on what was on the screen to go there first, like he usually did.

"Oooohhhh…," he muttered to himself. "Look, Bodi. Oh my God—it's got *comments*!"

Peter had taken an English 1A course—essay writing. The first essay he'd written, the autobiographical essay, had talked about Michael. The professor had adored it, had shared it with her classes, and then had told Peter that he should clean it up and submit it somewhere. The student creative writing periodical had rejected it, and he'd walked around with his shoulders slumped for three days before Bodi got him to confess. When he'd finally managed to put some words to his disappointment—"I really wanted the world to know him, is that so fucking wrong?"—Bodi had surprised him.

"Peter, that's not the only place you can send it. In fact, it's not even the best place. Daisy is seventy-five miles away—do you really think people want to see something so close to home look so ugly?"

So Peter had gone online and looked for places that seemed not to care about offending religion or politicians or whoever. He looked for places that seemed to tell the truth as he saw it and not the truth as the rule makers and the church people wanted the world to see it.

And now he was being published.

And Michael's story, and Bodi's, and Juliet's, and his mother's, and his—they would all be told. It would not be a dirty little secret in a town nobody had heard about. It would be a real tragedy, one he and Bodi had lived through with their hearts intact.

"Oooh…." Bodi's voice got low and mean. "That one asshole's gotta just fucking *quit*!"

Peter looked at the comment, which told him that he was going to hell and that Michael would burn there next to him, and flinched, and then recovered.

"It's nothing that the people we grew up with haven't told us all our lives," he said quietly, rubbing the small of Bodi's back, which always seemed to calm him down.

"Yeah, but—"

"Look at all these others," Peter said, excited by the turnout. "Look at them, Bodi. They're"—his voice caught—"they're sympathetic. Look. This one guy joined the military for the same reason."

Bodi's eyes scanned the text, which was not easy for him, but he got to the end and sighed. "Yeah," he said thickly. "I can't read many more of those replies."

Peter nodded, his own chest tight. "Me neither," he admitted. "But that's not the point. The point is...."

"They'll remember," Bodi said, his eyes bright in the reflection from the computer screen. "They'll remember. Michael will be remembered. Maybe someone will think about him when something like this comes up, and maybe they'll back the hell off."

"Exactly," Peter said softly. "Maybe someday, it won't have to be a tragedy to be gay, you know? Wouldn't it be awesome someday, if it just *was*?"

Bodi nodded and then captured his mouth in a kiss that escalated, forcing Peter to open his mouth and let Bodi inside to taste. Peter groaned and pulled back.

"Bodi," he whined, "I gotta... you know... shower. Brush my teeth... go to the bathroom...."

Bodi smiled and groped Peter's cock through his sleep shorts, then smiled wickedly. "That's not gonna be easy like this."

Peter grinned back, even though he knew he was flushing. He wasn't used to being able to play with Bodi like this, but God, he would enjoy it until the day he died.

"I'll do my best," he said, going for dignity. "If we're going to spend part of our day off in bed, I'm going to smell decent."

Bodi grinned. "Slacker," he said. "I showered before I woke you up. But I couldn't let you sleep, though. It was just too damned cool."

Peter looked down and smiled shyly, biting his lower lip. "It was okay?"

"Oh yeah," Bodi said reverently. Then, completely serious: "Don't you see what you did, Peter?"

Peter shook his head, and Bodi sighed.

"You made it *real*. Six years I lived here, alone, thinking I'd killed my sister, I'd driven Michael off, and Shawn told me I hadn't done anything wrong and my own head told me I hadn't done anything wrong, but *fuck* if it didn't feel like I'd done the whole damned thing because...." His hands moved restlessly, and his words pinwheeled for a moment, and he shook himself like the movement could get the thought across.

"Because. Because I may not have grown up all in Daisy, but my whole life was spent with people just like those people, and you believe the things you hear when you're young. And I really thought I was a bad person, and that's why all that bad shit happened. But it's not. You put it into words at Michael's funeral, and it stuck. And then you put it into words here, and it's sticking with more people." Bodi looked sad for a moment, and his eyes moved unhappily to his paintings, his artistic emotional slide to someplace that was better than his head had been for the past six years. His eyes moved back to Peter's face, his gaze close and personal and, thank God, happy.

"It's important, okay? It's important that it's in words. That people know. That whole week after you came and told me? I lived my whole life over again in that week, and you made it worth living, and you made the good parts real and the bad parts livable, and if you hadn't done that...." He shook his head. "I had to believe I was worth something to come back for you, Peter. And...." He compressed his mouth and then just kissed Peter again, hard.

Peter groaned, thrust his hands under Bodi's T-shirt to touch his stomach, and tried very hard not to just lie back in the computer chair and let Bodi ravish him as Bodi saw fit.

Bodi shook his head, though, and stepped back, pulling Peter's hands out of his shirt and putting his own hands virtuously behind him.

"Take your shower," he said, nodding. "Take your shower, and then I'll feed you breakfast, and then we can do anything we want. Shawn's got the garage today, and we can do anything we want." He grinned then, as gleeful as a child's kite at the shore.

"You set us free, Peter. We really do have the world at our feet."

Peter growled. "I'll be happy when I have you on your knees, sucking me off," he said, but he didn't mean it, and Bodi's grin was everything he needed to see.

Bodi kept his hands behind him and then moved in for one more less-than-virtuous kiss. This time when he pulled back, Peter was drugged from the kissing, his skin was quivering, his groin tingled, and he wanted to touch Bodi's stringy, pale-gold body with everything in him.

"Go shower, baby," Bodi told him, bending carefully and mouthing Peter's hardening cock through his underwear. "I waited six years for you. The least you can do is wait twenty minutes so we can make this right."

He turned around then and went to the kitchen, and Peter stood up, moaning in mock pain. "It'd be righter if we were naked!" he called, but he moved to the shower just the same. If Bodi wanted to make this special, well, Bodi had made every day of the last year special, from the moment he'd come busting in on Daisy's most sacred of grounds to now, when Peter headed for the shower and thought that he knew what real sacred ground was.

Real sacred ground was where you were loved. When Peter walked up the stairs every day to the little apartment above the garage, he was walking to Bodi, who loved him with as much truth and as much conviction as one person had ever loved another. When Peter walked through that door, he was done with mourning heaven, and living it instead.

AMY LANE is a mother of four and a compulsive knitter who writes because she can't silence the voices in her head. She adores cats, knitting socks, and hawt menz, and she dislikes moths, cat boxes, and knuckle-headed macspazzmatrons. She is rarely found cooking, cleaning, or doing domestic chores, but she has been known to knit up an emergency hat/blanket/pair of socks for any occasion whatsoever or sometimes for no reason at all. She writes in the shower, while commuting, while taxiing children to soccer/dance/karate/oh my! and has learned from necessity to type like the wind. She lives in a spider-infested, crumbling house in a shoddy suburb and counts on her beloved Mate, Mack, to keep her tethered to reality—which he does while keeping her cell phone charged as a bonus. She's been married for twenty-plus years and still believes in Twu Wuv, with a capital Twu and a capital Wuv, and she doesn't see any reason at all for that to change.

Visit Amy's website at http://www.greenshill.com. You can e-mail her at amylane@greenshill.com.

KEEPING PROMISE ROCK

http://www.dreamspinnerpress.com

GREEN'S HILL

http://www.dreamspinnerpress.com

Romance from AMY LANE

Romance from AMY LANE

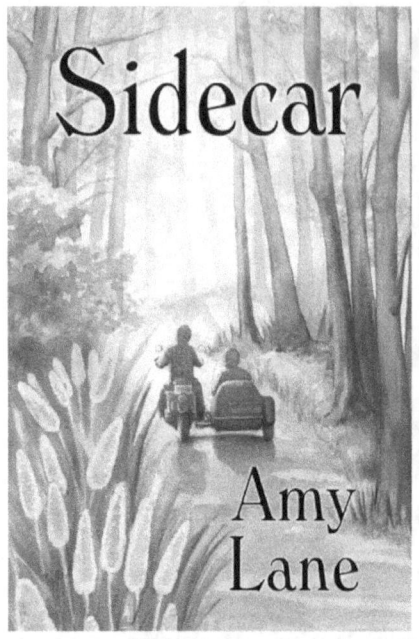
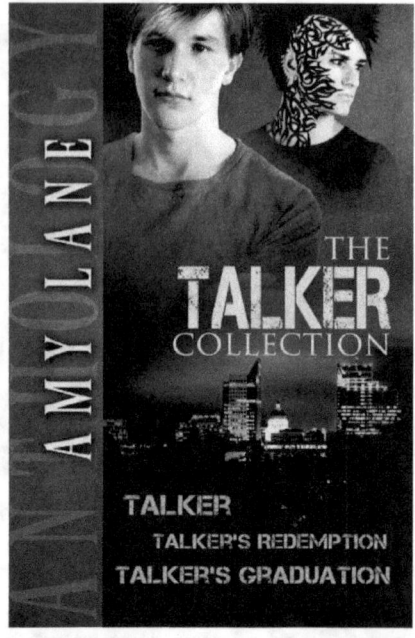

http://www.dreamspinnerpress.com

Romance from AMY LANE

http://www.dreamspinnerpress.com